THE NIGHT AT THE END OF THE TUNNEL

A SELECTION OF STRANGE SHORT STORIES

BY

MARTIN GOOCH

THE NIGHT AT THE END OF THE TUNNEL

A SELECTION OF STRANGE SHORT STORIES

A book of thoughts, thinks & things

Published by

Martin Gooch and his Gothic Manor

Gothic Manor Ltd.

Suite 86, 77 Beak Street

Soho

London

W1F 9DB

www.martingooch.com

"Esme and the Evil Aurora" Cover Art by Martin Gooch.

"Underground Workers" Original art by Vicky Stonebridge

PLEASE STAND BY

“Oh, where am I supposed to be then?” asked Frond.

I was very lucky to have had three
really brilliant teachers at school.
Mr. Berry, Mr. Beard and Mr. Carberry.
(English, Art and History)
Gentlemen, this is for you.

Contents:

Short stories:

Very Short Stories

Short Graphic Novels

Poems

The End

Introduction the 1st

Hello. Good evening.

And welcome to the book.

This book is a collection of short stories, thoughts, thinks and things (mostly things) that I've written over the last decade and a half or so, and is a companion to my short films script book (and DVD available now!).

Included are some short stories I wrote for adults and a couple I wrote for kids, as well as a few other things and a very short Graphic Novel that I am very fond of.

This book is full of a whole load of stuff that I hope will interest you, entertain you and maybe even inspire you to go and do something creative because without creativity the world would be a pretty dull place.

But probably cleaner.

And there would be less nuclear bombs and pollution and all that icky stuff.

Less machine guns. And less tax evasion, too.

Less taxes for that matter. I mean – most of them *are* a work of fiction!

Bollox.

Clearly everything bad in the world is the result of someone being creative.

But also everything good!

A work of art, in any form: a really good cheese sandwich on thick white bread, a flying boat, a super cool pair of sun glasses or even a beautiful moving story that makes you cry, but leaves you feeling wonderful!

Now *that* is creativity and I hope that maybe in some small way I can help you get closer to the good stuff.

And if all else fails, then give the book to someone with a wood burner.

They'll thank you for it when society collapses.

What to do if society collapses whilst reading this book.

If society collapses whilst you are reading this book then either:

a) Finish the book.

Or:

b) Don't finish the book.

If you chose a) and do finish the book then once you have finished the book, have a look out of what is left of your window and see what state the world is in and either:

c) Start the book again.

Or:

d) Don't start the book again.

If you choose c) then repeat until society is back how you like it or you are no longer able to continue reading the book in which case choose:

e) Death.

If you chose b) or d) and not to finish the book in the first place then have a look outside and decide whether to join in the Anarchy and set up a New World Order or join a whole load of mad max-esque post apocalyptic weirdoes with various items of sports equipment to act as armour and weld a spike on your car. That's probably the best you can do until order is restored.

Personally I have always fancied the post apocalyptic world, as you can obviously go over to the bloke who has really been annoying you for the last 5 years and smash his face in without much fear of going to prison. However he might just shoot you, so if you are going to do this, then make sure you fix him (or her) good first.

Don't forget that when you are setting up the new society to try and do something about good and bad, as that is invariably where we go wrong, and we get all confused with money and start thinking that bad people with a lot of money are actually good, and good people with no money are actually bad.

This is clearly wrong.

Remember – just because someone travels First Class, DOES NOT mean they are a First Class person.

So keep an eye on it as your new society forms.

If someone is an arsehole it's probably because they are an arsehole and has got nothing to do with what their mum or dad did or didn't do. They are just using their back-story as an excuse to be an arsehole.

Shoot them now to avoid having to do it later.

Other than that it's probably up to you.

Introduction the 2nd

I read all the time. I love it. I've always wanted to be a writer and specifically a fiction writer.

Some writers complain of writer's block, I usually have the opposite and paring down, or deciding, which idea I want to concentrate on can be quite tricky. Ideas float around for ages, like rogue butterflies – in vision but out of reach. They can flutter around for years, disappearing and then coming back in to view at the right moment. But it's only a moment and if I can't catch them then they are gone.

I always have a notebook in my jacket pocket, so I can scribble down fleeting thoughts whenever I am more than a dozen yards from a keyboard. I have a file on the computer labelled 'ideas' and I have a huge pile of half-full pieces of paper on my desk, with snatches of conversation, half formed thoughts, interesting words and sayings.

Isolating an idea is a pretty Herculean task, but once I have the idea further honing is required to identify what it is about the idea I want to write about. I like weird stuff, where the boundary between this world, here and now, is smudged with an else-world, another dimension or another time.

We know this world - our world - well but to open your mind to other possibilities surely must open the story gates to an almost infinite number of options?

But above all I need comedy. I love to read funny stuff. Most of the films I have written have been comedy and virtually all the films I have directed and written have had elements of comedy in them.

It's just the way my brain was wired up. Some people can't write comedy. Some people can't direct comedy, and being a sensitive soul and an empath, I probably couldn't write depressing true-life books/films of hardship or dreadful biographies of woe and evil people, without redemption.

Because oddly – they depress me. I couldn't pretend that in the heart of the human condition and psyche that there wasn't any relief or comedic gene on which to grow. All the evil in the world, corrupting and spoiling all the decent stuff, I don't believe it. I think somewhere something funny is going on.

This is all part of why I ended up in the film industry – that desire to go somewhere different, to merge reality and fiction, to go to fantastical places.

In far-fetched fiction, we are quite happy with a castle on a cloud. No problem. But in 'real fiction' people need to know why it's there, why it doesn't fall through the cloud, where the sewage goes, and how people get to work. Do they have little cloud cars or what?

That's not really logic, that's the world. Set up the far fetched world properly and the audience will believe you and buy it. No explanation of sewage required.

People, who like this sort of stuff, like this sort of stuff. Sometimes I feel I have to justify why I like to write the things I like to write, but really it's because I like to write them. I hope you like them too!

Thanks for reading.

Martin

Somewhere in North London 2014

PLANET DEUX

A sci-fi short story.

Annoyingly, it was found by the French.

An astronomer called Pierre! Pierre? I mean, come on, you couldn't make it up.

They unimaginatively named it 'Planet Deux', which was triple annoying as it was sort of half English sounding with the 'planet' bit at the front, and then with the very French sounding 'deux' at the end, which sort of gave the game away that it wasn't NASA who had found this bloody great lump of rock hanging in the cosmos.

It was also annoying, as it wasn't a very imaginative name - I mean planet two? Come on! Hardly the stuff of romance! What's wrong with the Greek or Roman Gods, we haven't run out you know, there is in fact a surfeit of gods ready to give their name to an interesting celestial body or two.

What about planet Thor or Valhalla? "We are proud to announce the existence of Valhalla!" that would have been brilliant!

But no. Planet bloody Deux it was.

And lastly it was triple annoying as it was the French. I don't wish to be racists at all, but they don't have a reputation for being smug bastards for nothing you know. I mean stereotypes are always based on fact. Know who the 'sausage eaters' are? That's right – The Germans who traditionally eat a lot of sausages.

What about 'Le Roast Beef'? Who might they be one wonders? Why it's the English who traditionally eat roast beef on a fairly common basis.

Or even the potato eaters? Indeed the country who eat a lot of potatoes, is it racist to base something on fact?

But no, I digress, it was also fourthly (if there is such a word, but I am sure you know what I mean) annoying because everyone else peering at the heavens through their incredibly expensive looking devices had missed it.

The French astronomers officially announced it at a conference of the European Space Commission in Paris. Yes, Paris, talk about milking an opportunity, and took great delight in telling the world of Planet Deux.

It was an Earth-like-planet surprisingly close to us, in orbit around a star that was very similar to The Sun, on the other side of the milky way to us – almost a 'mirror image' scoffed one scientist from Belgium who went on to make a joke about the French needing to check for 'reflections and refractions', which was probably hilarious if you spent your life on your own looking at data on colour shift and polarity procession.

But exist it did. Planet Deux was clearly there for all to see, well for all who had a bloody massive telescope to see.

They pointed the Hubble telescope in the right direction and after a couple of attempts got the co-ordinates and focus right and there was a picture of this pale blue-ish dot, with all white clouds wiggling across the surface just like, well, just like Planet Une – Earth.

It was very difficult to see the surface of the planet as there was so much cloud cover and the planet appeared to have a large body or bodies of water swishing about on the surface.

The scientists were getting excited, and the story even made it in to the tabloids, admittedly on page 17, just below the story about the woman who had had a sex change and married her neighbour, who had also had a sex change. Twice.

They (the scientists, not the woman with the sex change) used thermal imagining, radio telescopes, isometric pressure gauges and they even reversed the polarity a couple of times, until someone pointed out that if you reveres the polarity twice then you are back with your original polarity.

And eventually after a great deal of data had been crunched and assessed and then crunched again a map of the surface of the planet began to form.

Some unhinged individuals, conspiracy theorist and the type had been predicting portents of doom, that we had been looking upon the Earth itself somehow projected in the future, and we hadn't recognized it as the polar ice caps would have melted and thus the landscape would be almost unrecognizable due to the rise of the seas and the obliteration of the coast lines.

But what the scientists saw on the clever computer maps was a largely brown planet, below the white clouds, and apart from the blue seas – the Equator covered by a huge belt of desert three thousand miles from the north to the south. Non-existent ice caps, and three large oceans but not nearly as large as the Pacific or Atlantic or even the Indian Ocean for that matter.

It was a burnt, hot, planet, they could clearly see where great oceans, like on Mars had once filled up the planet, and the clever geologists pointed to huge carvings in the landscape that 'could only have been caused by the movement of Glaciers'.

There was debatable evidence of once great forests and tundra that may have covered the planet at one point, but not any more.

'Forests?' laughed the Belgium scientist again, 'maybe' he said 'They were confusing their beeches with their benches' which got a few laughs but he was really pushing it now.

And then they found it.

It was a burst of radiation.

But that's not uncommon in space.

What was interesting was that is was a very specific burst of radiation – a Strontium 90, which only occurs when atoms are exploded.

Something that doesn't occur, without the helping hand of technology and therefore: the helping hand of a *sentient* being.

'Gulp' said the scientists, cause this meant that who ever had lived or lived on Planet Deux had split the atom, at least once and therefore had nuclear capabilities, and maybe that meant they had starships and maybe that meant that they had telescopes and maybe that meant that they might be looking for another planet to inhabit as well?

But they were a long way away and "are we scared of little green men?" scoffed a very important politician in a nice blue suit, with his own aircraft parked, fuelled and with a bomb shelter programmed into the sat-nav.

'Well, yes," said a lot of people, we are scared of 'little green men.'

'After all,', they continued, 'Uncle Frank was abducted last year and has never been the same since – and someone killed all the chickens, admittedly it could have been a fox, but there were some weird lights a week before, so you never know."

Whilst all that was going on, those clever French chaps had been working away with a really decent computer about projection, gravitation and cosmic shift and all that, and tried to play back time to work out where this particular star system had travelled from.

After all, we are all travelling in space, and if you can plot things back a bit, then you can see where the planet was formed, where it was 'born' and if it was a neighbour or not.

More, and better, photos came back from the new improved Hubble Mark II and it was clear that this planet had signs of life. It didn't look so great – one prominent science fiction writer of the time said it was probably a good idea to leave this planet alone, but as he was a 'fiction' writer everyone ignore him, because 'The opinions of dreamers are not the opinions of the people' as one newspaper put it.

Tell that to Karl Marx, John Lennon, Jesus Chris or Adolf Hitler. Actually, not Hitler, he's a bad example.

Dreamers like civil engineers, artists, writers, oh yeah and nuclear physicists who can dream up things like the thing we appeared to be running away from now…

Planet Deux had clearly some sort of major life forms as there were the remains of cities, better than the canals on mars and even the evidence of a once great war – craters and heavy radiation and destruction on a planet wide scale.

The scientists who knew about this sort of thing made a calculation based on the half life of various isotopes and things like that and made an assumption that the major destruction on the planet had happened about 'give or take' a thousand Earth years before.

A long time - but not so long in geological and cosmic times.

A decision was made to send a probe.

It'd take a few years to build and design and all that stuff, but then a super clever bloke from the space agency said "can't we re-direct' a satellite that's already en-route?'

They looked and checked and found a Russian probe that almost everyone had forgotten about (including the Russians) that was heading in almost the right direction, and with a few bursts of it's retro's to turn it around and get a bit of sun on it's solar panels, some new software updates and programs and it was, almost, good to go.

And off it went.

It is amazing how actions cause ripples, 'cause and effect' I suppose they would call it. Cause only one person found the Russian probe, as it was top secret, and if he hadn't re-discovered it, it would probably have been over looked, and another probe would have been selected, or even drawn up and blasted off into space.

But it wasn't and they didn't cause they had the Russian one.

Anxious ears and even more anxious eyes watched many computer screens across Planet earth as the Russian probe Andropov 9 finally approached Planet Deux 3 years later.

A lot of work had obviously been done since then: Earth scientists had tried to contact the inhabitants of the planet, but they had steadfastly refused to reply or even acknowledge any of the transmissions and stubbornly refused to show themselves, even though evidence of civilizations on the planet was incontrovertible. There clearly had been a civilization on the planet but where had they all gone?

The people of Earth waited expectantly for the first decent close up pictures from the probe.

And then finally on the 11th of May 2072 the probe got close enough to unfurl its weird antennae thing and start taking pictures. It approached Planet Deux, and did a high equatorial orbit, and then it did a polar orbit to be sure, and then it began its descent.

The photos at 1 mile up showed all the usual stuff – clouds, seas, continents, all that, as the scientists from Earth had seen via the Hubble Mk II, and as the probe descended on its equatorial descent it took more photos which were immediately compared and contrasted with the ones from the higher orbits, any differences would mean that there had been movement on the surface of the planet.

Half a mile up - and the photos coming back showed huge cities that had been laid waste, but no signs of active life at all.

200,000ft up and it was possible to see interesting bits of infrastructure – what appeared to be huge ships of some sort, destroyed in harbours, and things that looked very much like roads criss-crossed the planet.

100,000ft up the Russian Probe whizzed past what was unquestionably a satellite, but as the probe was travelling at a rate of 15,000 miles an hour, the readings were unclear. Scientists on Earth High-Fived each other!

At 35,000 feet, a scientist on Earth noticed a difference between two orbit pictures: Something had moved…

At 20,000 feet the probe reported that some sort of tracking device had locked onto it, and at 15,000 it could see the missiles heading towards it.

At 13,257ft the probe was destroyed in an enormous thermo nuclear blast, which even the boys working the Hubble Mk II could see.

"Oh dear," said the Earth Scientists.

"Oh shit," and, "I told you so," said the Science Fiction writer back on Earth who had been watching the live transmission on TV, as had most of the 12 billion people on the planet.

*

After some hurried analysis of all the data sent back from the probe, prior to its demise, the scientist concluded that the arrival of the Russian Probe had set off a nuclear response from the long dead planet. It was in fact a massive salvo of nuclear missiles equipped to fly deep space, launched from all over the planet, North, South, East and West, a positive buzzing angry hornet's nest of missiles.

It appeared that the planet had indeed been wiped of all life by the previous inhabitants during a war over who knew what, and the remaining missiles had been sitting there quietly biding their time until an object approached them at great speed.

Then they would launch, destroy it, and calculate the origin of the missile, or in our case, the probe, and send a large number of massive planet bursting nuclear missiles back as a special present for whoever sent the missile in the first place.

All the way back to Earth…

As almost all funding to NASA had been cut decades ago - there are no shuttles left, and nobody ever started work on deep space craft. The Russians have been busy trying to dig huge underground factories and steal everyone else's fuel sources, whilst the Chinese have been too busy building washing machines and play stations to bother with anything that went further out than a communications satellite.

Nobody knows what to do – though it's pretty clear that Judgment day is coming and we know the date.

There was talk about the RAF shooting the missiles down once they entered the atmosphere, but by the time they get here they will be travelling at almost 1,200,000 miles per hour, and there are 13,428 of them, some of which, it is speculated, contain multiple warheads, which will be launched as they hit the upper atmosphere.

Enough to 'split the planet in half,' as one helpful scientist pointed out.

There is a lot of anti-French feeling, as everyone feels it's their fault: if they hadn't been so smug about it, and just left it well alone, then none of this would have happened.

Many people feel we should have a war with France just for the hell of it, but nobody can really be arsed. I mean a war is a lot of work, and we really should be concentrating, on getting everyone to Mars or at least to the Moon, where we could watch the greatest fireworks display in history go off.

One scientist has predicted that most of the water in the oceans will be boiled off, into space as the atmosphere is ripped from the planet, as all the oxygen is used up by the nuclear fireball which will engulf the Earth - so those clever politicians who think they can survive the whole thing in commandeered nuclear submarines are out of luck, which is of some cold comfort to the man in the street, who really doesn't want to die alone.

I'm working on one of these rushed Government projects to build space habitats that will just be floating in orbit to hopefully keep a few people alive, but it's very hard to get motivated to come to work, as I have a feeling I'm not building it for me…

And how long will it have to stay in space before it is safe to come back to Earth? A generation? Two? Ten? A hundred?

It doesn't seem very positive to me. I'm tempted to join the End of the World Alliance, a bunch of Hippies who have moved to the seaside and are drinking, smoking and shagging themselves to death, I can probably enjoy some of that.

What do *you* think we should do?

They'll be here in 3 years, 201 days and counting.

The End

ESME AND THE EVIL AURORA

By Martin Gooch

(Aged 36 & nine twelfths)

Chapter 1

The Artists Commune

Once upon a time, not so far away, there was an Artists' Commune by the sea. And on this Artists Commune lived a little girl called Esme.

It was a nice commune and Esme was a nice girl. A big bob of white blonde hair gave her a shadow that sometimes looked like a dandelion. Or possibly a poppy, or even a seedpod. She also had two large leaves growing out of her forehead which…no.

She didn't. I'm just being silly.

No one ever actually called her Pod head or Dandelion shadow, they all actually called her Esme, except for one person who called her Ebola, but that's another story.

So Esme was her name and shall remain so at least for the length of this story.

She had grown into a striking woman but scared many people away as her right eye was bright red and her left eye pitch black. It was dis-concerting for those who did not know her – and for those that did it sometimes felt like she was looking into your very soul. They felt their skin being peeled away as she looked into their very hearts to see what made them tick…

Of course everyone knew who she was in the village – how could you miss the striking white haired woman with the soul searching stare? And of course she had lived there her whole life…

Esme spent a lot of her time thinking, for the Artists Commune was a thinker's paradise. Willows willowed in the wind and water lapped at the shore. Apart from her pet, a single black and white bunny called Verminthrax, (that was actually a robot, and powered itself by gnawing through electric cables. It was spying on Esme for an evil foreign government, but that's not important now), who lived in a hutch in the hall, Esme lived on her own, in a little wooden lodge, that was not far from the rest of the village.

It was a fab little artists' residence, which had views over the rolling waters and ample opportunity to observer the passing water life, and a good view of Captain Mart's Tower of Confusion, a strange almost organic tower that seemed to grow from the rocky ground from which it stood, nestled neatly at the corner of the cove.

The commune was situated deep within a hidden cove and was seldom interfered with by the outside world. A single bridge spanned the deep waters to the mainland, but the far side was shrouded in mist and few people ever made the journey to the far side, preferring to rely on the regular visits from the post man and the deliverers of internet shopping.

A lot of the people on the island were quite odd. That's what happens on islands generally, people become a bit odd. It's all to do with the isolation, and the fact that the sort of people who like to live on an island are often quite odd, so it's a sort of self-fulfilling prophecy!

Esme's mum and dad were quite odd, and eventually left for a round the world airship cruise. They left Esme with instructions on when to pay the milkman, and when the bin men came. But they never came back. Esme was not that surprised because they had packed up all their stuff and forwarded it to another address and put a not unpleasant amount of money in her bank account.

Esme always felt it might be something to do with her dad's dreadful business decisions and gambling, but things had worked out OK after a long bit of sadness, and besides other interesting things happened on the island.

There was old Gilgamesh who grew strange flowers in his garden that watched you, like eyes on a portrait, as you walked past. Mrs. Sykes who was perfecting the hoop shaped sandwich, you could wear on your wrist until it was lunchtime, and of course the wonderful Captain Mart. What he was a captain of, no one was quite sure, but that he *was* a captain everyone *was* sure of.

Captain Mart worked on many strange projects and spent a while projecting evil faces onto clouds that looked like a satanic aurora borealis. He said he was doing it to put people coming off coming to live on the island, which everyone was agreed was a good idea as they all liked it there and didn't want anyone coming and spoiling it. Esme liked to go to the cliffs and sit and watch Captain Mart's aerial projections. It helped her think.

Esme spent a lot of time thinking, because she had a lot of time to spend. Rather unfortunately she had been cursed by fairly annoying Gods, to forever be thinking about stuff. And as a result, she could never clear her brain and go to sleep. Try as she might, she just couldn't get sex out of her mind, I mean, go to sleep.

She'd tried all sorts of potions and lotions and suggestions, but to no avail. She just could not doze off.

Extra pillows and eiderdowns were located. A special mattress and soft sheets were purloined. Even a special perfume was ordered all the way from Paris, that purportedly 'aided restful slumber', but it didn't.

One early morning, very much like the one we had today, Esme despondedly pulled open her front door, skipped lightly (but miserably) down the 13-and-a-half steps and wandered into one of the commune's small shops to buy some printer ink.

The door 'tinkled' as she entered the shop, as all good small shop doors should do. Obviously it's the bell 'tinkling' not the door, but you get my meaning.

"Good Morning Miss Esme," said Mr. Love the Communes Printer Ink specialist, "what," he continued, "can I do for you today?" he beamed. Beaming nicely cleaned teeth.

"Oh," sighed Esme, "Just another score of ink cartridges," she replied, "I've got to send my latest epic off to my agent, and these cartridges only have about enough ink in them for about two pages."

"Very true," said Mr. Love. And he turned to his hugely stacked shelves, whistling as he did so.

Esme pondered on the content of Mr Love's shop as Mr. Love located the cartridges. Books and boxes, cartridges and cans, pens and peas, tea and talc. All needs catered for!

"Here we are!" Exclaimed Mr. Love, off loading an armful of cartridges into Esme's shopping sack. Money was exchanged. Changed, received and soon Esme was on her way along the little alleyway back to her lodge.

Just as she was about to turn into her little gate, Ivan from number 33 came wandering past and offered Esme a cheery wave and a cheeky wink, or possibly a cheeky wave and cheery wink, it was always so hard to tell with Ivan…

"Printing again?" Inquired Ivan.

"All done, this one: off to the agent tomorrow!"

"Great! Er, have you got any of those veggie sausages left? Only I'm running a bit low?"

"Ha ha. No," said Esme firmly, sliding through her gate and running up the steps to the sanctuary of her domicile, slamming the door behind her. Ivan's love of veggie sausages was known island-wide, and one had to be careful to maintain a satisfactory veggie sausage supply.

Ivan realised that to have any success with his Ouija board and his attempts to contact the dead probably really needed a live sacrifice, but as he was a vegetarian, he was travelling around in a cul-de-sac of failure. His endless sacrifices of veggie sausages had so far elicited not a single 'peep' from the dead.

But he was not a man to give up and many more veggie sausages would, needlessly, be sacrificed by his hand in the years to come.

All this watched by a sharp eyed crow, perched upon a dusty skull at the foot of Esme's garden.

Chapter 2

A nights printing

Esme printed away for all her heart was worth and as the pages chattered out of her antiquated printer, the sun set and the moon rose, casting a glittering silver shadow across the inky waters surrounding her Artists' Commune.

Hardly noticing that another day had gone, Esme looked at her new manuscript and spotted a typo on page 3, so had to start printing out again.

"Bugger." She said, and then, "Fuck it!" Because this isn't really a children's story and therefore fucking swearing is allowed, for fuck's sake. Fuck.

The printer chattered some more and soon it was time for tea. Esme sleepily shuffled into the kitchen to embark on a tea making mission, but calamity! The fridge was bare! Apart from the butter, eggs, fish, side of roast boar, bottle of gin and jar of bumberry jam there was no weird tea! Oh how the heavens taunted Esme with these dastardly devious devices.

Esme's head hung. 'Mr. Love's,' she said. And sure enough, dragging on her big rubber thigh high kinky boots she trudged off in the morning mists to Mr. Love's shop.

Ding dong, dinged the door dinger. Esme wandered up to the counter where Mr. Love stood silently, seemingly gazing into the middle distance, wherever that may be.

"Hello Mr. Love," greeted Esme.

Mr. Love made no reply.

Esme furrowed her brow. "Hello Mr. Love." She repeated.

Still no movement from Mr. Love.

"Weird tea please."

Nothing.

Esme thought she would try the magic words: "I've got CASH," she said loudly.

Mr. Love's head turned with unseeing eyes in Esme's direction. As he moved, Esme became aware of a strange rhythmic sound. Tick tock. Tick tock. It went, and indeed: tick tock again.

Esme cocked her head, which is easier to say than do.

Tick tock. Tick tock. Very odd it was too. Mr. Love turned and headed for the lone glass fronted fridge, where he located a box of weird tea and returned to Esme.

Esme offered over some grubby coins, which Mr. Love vacantly took, and rung up in the till.

Mr. Love resumed his silent staring stance silently. Esme took her leave, grasping her weird tea to her ample bosom.

She hurried along the little alley, only to see Ivan the commune's Ouija board expert, striding towards her, with the air of a man with a mission. Esme was just about to greet Ivan, when she saw the now familiar thousand yard stare and heard the accompanying tick tock. Tick tock.

"…Ivan…?" was all she could muster as Ivan strode up to and past the almost trembling Esme.

Esme hurried home and made her disgusting tea.

'What on earth could be going on?' wondered the alarmed Esme. Just then, there came a double ding ding from the front door bell.

Not expecting a visitor, Esme was slightly surprised to find her neighbour Miss Sairah, tearfully standing on her doorstep. "Oh Esme!" wailed Miss Sairah, "It's my Thorven, he's gone all funny! I don't know what to do!"

Never being one to miss a trick, young Esme immediately saw the connection: "Is he silent?" Asked Esme.

Miss Sairah nodded as she blew into her snotty hanky.

"Staring into the middle distance, where-ever that may be?"

More nodding and nose blowing.

"Ticking and a tocking?"

"Yes," wailed Miss Sairah, as she threw her arms around Esme.

Chapter 3

Tick tock. Tick tock.

A few moments later saw Esme and Miss Sairah standing by the side of Miss Sairah's Thorven, who was lying in bed, staring up vacantly at the ceiling.

"Thorven!" called Esme loudly. Her word, the only sound apart from the regular tick tock. Tick tock coming from Thorven's barrel chest. But response from Thorven came there none.

"Weird," said Esme.

"And look at this," gestured Miss Sairah with a shaking digit, indicating Thorven's pyjama top.

Hesitantly Esme undid the top three buttons and pulled apart the two sides of the pyjama top.

Esme gasped.

Right down the middle of Thorven's chest was a very neat, almost beautifully crafted scar, sewn up with tiny stitches that even the finest surgeon in the cove would have had difficultly surgeoning.

"Crumbs," exclaimed Esme, inspecting the stitches and scar closely. "This is fine work indeed!"

"Fine work? Fine work?" I don't bloody care how good a job they did! I want to know what has happened to my Thorven!"

Esme returned to her lodge to ponder the strange events of the morning. Only to be disturbed several times by other commune members. It seemed that almost half the cove had woken to find the other half vacant and ticking.

"Curiouser and fucking curioser," exclaimed Esme who had never liked Alice, as she felt it could have done with a re-write and didn't address the wants and needs of the Red queen in enough depth. "She was the real hero of the story," spouted Esme rather obtusely.

Another night of sleeplessness passed. Esme finished her printing, wrote a neat little note and bundled it all up in brown paper and string ready for the postie the following ay-em. Then she spent ten minutes making a video art thing and did a couple of plans for her next art installation project.

Postie arrived exactly on cue. The house moo-coo clock had only just begun to moo the nine o-clock hour when the front door bell ding-ding a dinged.

“Ah, hello Postie…” began Esme as she opened her door, parcelled manuscript in hand. But then she stopped.

Standing in the door way was the Postie, but it was a vacant Postie. And a tick tocking Postie at that.

The Postie stuck out his hand in a movement that any expert in the field of Robotic dancing would have been extremely impressed with.

Esme carefully placed her parcel in the Postie’s grey hand.

The Postie turned an unseeing head in Esme’s directing and raised his other hand.

Esme jumped back. But then realised what the Postie meant and rummaging around in her small purse rapidly thrust several even grubbier coins into the damp palm of the silent Postie.

The Postie seemed to weigh up the parcel and the grubby coins and seeing that it was enough or even more than enough, thrust the parcel into his large leather sack and turning on a sixpence, strode off with a curious mechanical gait towards the small gate and off up the alley way.

Quickly returning to pick up the sixpence and pocket it, but all in the most robotic fashion that a Japanese Robot designer would have wept to see.

“Blimey,” said Esme and she was right.

At that moment the cove's only pilot zoomed overhead in his fantastic tri-plane. It was Captain Mart.

"He'll know what's going on," thought Esme.

And you know what?

She was right.

Chapter 4

Captain Mart's incredible Tri-Plane.

Captain Mart bought his incredible Tri-plane into land on the glass like smooth surface of the river. He cut the engine twenty feet above the water and an almost windless approach meant the huge pontoons slung low under the Captains Tri-plane touched the water with barely a sound.

Ripples spread out alarming pond-skaters and water vole, but apart from the splosh of water and the cooling engine 'plinks' it was silent. A duck quacked because it felt it should.

It was a beautiful landing and the Captain was already mooring the flying machine at the quayside at the foot of his Tower of Confusion when Esme came plodding along.

"Hello Captain," she began as an opening gambit, which was pretty standard in these sorts of conversations.

"Hi Esme," retorted the Captain who was well versed in how these sorts of things went.

"I have a question for you."

"Fire away!"

"Somehow people in the commune are having their hearts replaces with tick tocking ones… and…"

The good Captain's stopped tying up the floating Tri-plane and gave Esme his full attention, which was actually quite a lot when the Captain got down to it. "What do you mean 'tick tocking'?"

"The hearts make a tick tock sound like they are…clockwork or something…" Suggested Esme.

"Oh dear," said the Captain, heading to his tower door. "Probably indigestion," he suggested, "have they tried Mr. Peregrines' own Heartburn Relief? It's very good."

The Captain was half way into the door of his Tower of Confusion, when Esme interrupted.

"TEA!" she demanded. This usually resulted in Esme being invited in for the aforementioned tea, and if she was lucky a biscuit or two. (Sometimes three, and once even four!)

"Sorry," said the good Captain, "Tad busy." And so saying he firmly closed the lead lined tower door in the face of Esme.

"How odd," she said as she skipped back to her house. "The Captain never says no to my demands for tea!"

Esme stopped suddenly. She could hear the sound of Tick Tocking. She looked around.

There was no one there, neither up the communes' single lane, nor down.

She looked around with slightly more squinted eyes. She listened.

Esme breathed. The Triplane's engine 'plinked' again as it cooled. The willows willowed. A different duck quacked. A bumberry berry bush farted. There was no other sound.

She cocked her head again, which as I mentioned before is a sight to behold.

Tick tock. There it was again. Tick. Tock. Tick bloody tock. There was only one place it could have come from: There was a small window open in the east facing side of Captain Mart's Tower of Confusion.

Esme grabbed a garbage can from outside one of the neighbours and dragging over another four managed to construct an extremely hazardous climbing apparatus pyramid.

Just enough garbage cans for Esme to be able to scale the Tower of Confusion to the little open window on the first floor, and place her tiny nose on the windowsill.

Peering into the room, it took a moment for Esme's eyes to adjust to the gloom within the room. There was an air of doom, and she wished she had a zoom lens to take it all in.

The room was a very full workshop, shelf after shelf of books filled all the wall space. A weird chart on the wall, showed a dissected human torso…And every surface was full of little ticking devices.

Ticking devices.

Ticking.

And tocking.

In the middle of all these little heart sized devices was Captain Mart. Screw driver in hand.

He stood up, Esme crouched down.

"Perfection." He said. In front of him was a little tick tocking heart sized machine, only it wasn't ticking or tocking. It just sort of wobbled rhythmically without making any sound at all.

"No more noises!" he said! And with that Esme lost her balance on the Garbage cans: it's very difficult to keep your balance when using your nose as a support!

Especially such a small nose.

CRASH BANG and predictably WALLOP.

"SHIT!" screamed Esme as she fell to earth, and a moment later found herself staring up at the good Captain.

"What were you doing spying on me?" Asked the Captain eyebrow raised.

"I heard the ticking and I had to have a look."

"Curiosity…" Said the Captain enigmatically. Or at least he thought he was being enigmatic. If his friend, the 2nd lord of Innuendo, had been there: he would have thought Captain Mart said it like a nob.

"Why are you changing peoples hearts Captain Mart?"

Captain Mart opened his mouth to say something, then closed it, then opened it again: "Tea? I've got some custard creams in?"

Chapter 5

Tea and custard creams.

Ten minutes into the future saw Esme slouched in her favourite sloucher at a jaunty angle by Captain Mart's Mammoth tusk tea table.

The Captain enters with a splendid manticore hide tea tray, resplendent with a China tea set and a brace of unicorn horn spoons.

"There we are." He said placing the tea things onto the Mammoth tusk tea table.

"Once upon a time, my heart got broke," said Captain Mart, as he poured tea through the gold plated tea strainer, (having previously warmed the cup), "And it really hurt. Like fuck."

Captain Mart slurped at his mauve tea.

"…and then I only went and got it broke again, so I thought: Enough! If I could make a decent clockwork heart, then I'd never have to feel that sort of thing again."

Esme nodded: continue.

"So last week I perfected it or so I thought. I hadn't really noticed the tick tocking: you see I like to work with music on, but my neighbour complains, so I have to work with headphones. So I never really heard the noise…"

"But why did you change other peoples hearts?"

"Because I wanted them to be happy! They are always moaning! About the weather, the food, the floods, the cost of printer paper (at this he narrowed his eyes at Esme) and the strangers who come to the island! Why do you think I invented the Evil Aurora?

"To keep people away?"

"No – to make the people here think I was keeping people away! So they would be happier and have one less thing to moan about!

No. Their lives will be much better if they can't ever have a broken heart. No heart ache, No nothing."

"But no love. No compassion. No emotion. No feeling!!" preached Esme.

"So?" questioned Captain Mart.

"Life must have the bad, to really enjoy the good!" said Esme not entirely sure she believed what she was saying.

"That is bollox and you know it," said Captain Mart. "There are some people out there who live acceptable lives, fall in love, never have their hearts broken and are happy most of the time!"

"Bastards."

"Yeah, you're right. Bastards."

"Look, you need to replace Thorven's and Mr. Love and Ivan and everyone's hearts with their original ones." Esme took a custard cream. "It's up to them if they want to be unhappy or not. Not you."

The Captain sighed. Crestfallen. "OK. I just wanted everyone to not feel heat ache…"

"You promise you'll replace their hearts?" asked Esme munching on her custard cream. "Er. You have still got their hearts haven't you?"

"Yes, I kept them in case I ever felt someone needed to feel bad."

"Hmm," she hmmed, "I did wonder," she continued, "how you managed to do all these fiddly operations on your own?

"I used Ivan's Ouija board to summon small nimble spirits to help with the surgery. How did you think I did such tiny stitches?"

"I dunno. I kinda just thought it was magic," said Esme.

"Thanks," smiled Capt Mart.

"That wasn't a compliment," she scowled.

"Oh." Said the Captain and frowned.

He looked sad.

Esme felt a strange feeling. She should have felt happy that she had solved the mystery, but she knew someone's dreams and long thought plans were being unraveled. All because of her.

"Cheers then!" She beamed!

Esme and the Captain clinked their china teacups.

And munched their custard creams, as a flock of geese flew over head in an amazing 'V'. The timing couldn't have been better.

Chapter 6

All's well that ends…

"Hello Mr. Love," said Esme as she entered the commune's shop, "How are you?"

"Feeling much better thanks. Not been feeling myself for the last few days, but back to normal now."

"Glad to hear it."

"Just one thing Esme, what do you make of this?" Mr. Love unbuttoned the top two buttons of his checked shirt and revealed to Esme his manly chest.

Esme inspected. "Looks like a scar. A very neat one."

"Exactly. But I didn't have one last week!"

"A lot of girls go for scars you know…"

"…really?" stammered Mr. Love.

"Really!" winked Esme as she bounced out of the shop, leaving the money for her Goth Juice hair gel on the pile of newspapers under Mr. Love's nose.

Wandering down the alley Esme waved at Thorven, weeding in the garden, blew a kiss to Ivan, working in his studio and took the letters from the Postie with a smile.

Sitting on her steps was Captain Mart. He looked tired.

"I've done what you asked. Everyone's back to normal."

"Thank you!" Said Esme, giving the Captain a peck on the cheek, "Tea?"

"Thanks but no, I need to perfect the transperambulation of pseudo cosmic anti-matter before dinner. It'll help with the evil aurora projections. See you." The Captain got up and adjusted his jacket and began to leave.

Esme hugged him. The Captain smiled a sad smile and headed off back to his Tower of Confusion.

Esme smiled, but then cocked her head.

She could hear something.

She was sure.

A Tick tocking getting fainter as the Captain walked away.

THE END

THE DAY GOD CAME BACK

It was the year 2222, on the 22nd of February at 22:22 and 22 seconds when God, finally, decided to return.

He appeared simultaneously on all TVs across the world, on all media formats in all languages.

He also appeared in all cities and towns that began with a 'G' in an almost holographic appearance reminiscent of the great and powerful Oz from the Wizard of Oz.

There was smoke and flame of an appropriately biblical proportion and his voice boomed and echoed from the heavens as you hoped God's voice would.

The world ground to a sudden silent halt. Even pictures in magazines and paintings hung in galleries turned into God's face as he spoke.

It was, as spectacles go, spectacular on a grand scale hither-to unseen on Earth. (Or anywhere else in the Universe as far as we know).

"My Children," he began, "I'm, to put it mildly, disappointed," he continued.

The brighter humans gulped with an ominous fore-boding, as the glazed eyed worshipping members of the population stared slack jawed at their God and felt their minds empty of all rational thought, "You have befouled the wonderful Eden I created for you. And I am sad."

The world collectively held its polluted breath.

"You have ruined this planet, poisoned the water, stripped the sky, and ground the earth. You should be ashamed."

The world was, or at least the people were. The World itself didn't give a toss what was going on, what with it being made of rock and lava and all.

"But I am a kind and wise God, and I have created a new world for you far away in another Galaxy, (a Galaxy also created)," he said as an aside, "a world called New Eden," is what he said.

Personally I thought this was rather unimaginative – I mean this guy can create anything and the best name he can come up with is 'New Eden'? – I mean, like, come on.

"It's a wonderful world, twice as big, a little bit warmer, less dangerous animals, lower gravity, so things are easier to lift, I've worked out good and evil a bit better, and I've even done the Unicorn properly this time," he said, slightly smugly I felt.

Around the planet people nodded at their fellows, this sounds pretty good!

"But," continued Almighty God again, as the world collectively thought – "Uh-oh, here's the 'but'…"

"Even as powerful as I am I cannot transport all 20 stinking Billion of you. I wish I could but I can't… But… I can transport your souls…"

The first suicides had actually started as soon as God had appeared and had been steadily rising – but at this point a kind of madness gripped the population of the Earth and suicide reigned.

Funnily enough the Muslims, the followers of Islam, were the most keen to get to the next world and started killing themselves in droves.

Obviously killing yourself for your God was no biggie to these guys.

Those members of the Church of England seemed to be the most reticent to hand over their lives to get to the next world, but then so many of them lived really nice comfortable lives on the current planet they were inhabiting… It was hard to give up your nice big house, garden, shiny car, and heavily fortified walls.

The lowest deaths were in the Nordic Countries where even though the snow had been mostly stripped away a century ago, the dour temperament remained and they only lost 74% of the population.

Many aircraft failed to land successfully as air traffic control had stopped talking to them, some pilots just simply stopped flying, and closed their eyes.

Soldiers opened fire on their superiors sensing things were going wrong. They were right.

A technician in an ancient nuclear power station in what was once England, threw every switch and then jumped into the radioactive core causing the station to go critical and in doing so destroyed a square mile of the planet, taking thousands with him, and ending nuclear power for good.

Power stations across the globe failed and the lights went out. Plunging the world into powerless chaos.

In a single day the population of the world was halved.

God went on to say some other stuff and that the planet was doomed, and anyone still around in 40 days (and 40 nights, (must be a 'thing')) would be consumed by the rise of rats and roaches as the humans failed to cope with the tide of rotting corpses filling the streets.

It really was Hell on Earth. Those surviving religious leaders had a field day as they smugly felt everything they had been banging on about for centuries had been proven correct. That is until the rats began to nibble at their toes and then suddenly they realised that being smug was probably a sin as well. Bit late for that though.

The World was already in the middle of the 2nd Dirt War – which was a revolt from the people over the revolting situation most of the citizens of Earth found themselves in.

God had been right. We had ruined his Eden. Life expectancy was short, disease was high, technology and technological advance was a thing of the past as crippled governments sought to feed their people and try to keep a semblance of order, at the expense of science and progress.

Most species were extinct, no one had eaten meat for over 70 years – as all available land was given to agriculture. But we all knew it was futile, we had passed the point of no return. Quality of life was zero. Eden had died.

And as previous short-sighted governments had abolished all the space programs there was no way to get off planet, the long promised escape to the stars was nothing but a dream. Humanity was dying.

After the first Day of the Dead, as it came to be known, many people continued to commit suicide as they saw what little of society was left – disintegrate. All remaining services ceased and Anarchy was the new norm.

At the end of his message, God said he would return in the year 3333 to check up, but as he'd already said we only had 40 days, I put that down to a bad script editor, and him clearly making some of it up as he went along. Or maybe he was an old sentimentalist and just wanted to see how it all turned out. A bit like leaving an old oak tree in your garden even though you know it's dying…

Within a year the population of the planet stabilised at 1.5 billion people.

Sensibly God had nominated a representative on Earth called God's Emperor: She was a woman called Alexandra. She was already big in the New World Government and God decreed that she was now 'Boss of the World'. For life.

Obviously she was pretty busy for the first year – dealing with the utter chaos of the newly religious suicidally fanatic planet.

Bombings were daily as zealots helpfully took a whole load of souls with them to New Eden.

Cults performed mass suicides – the biggest in India where 500,000 people drank poison. They hadn't bothered to arrange any sort of clean up and that was a hell of a mess.

Emperor Alexandra had the whole area seeded with rapid growing weeds that transformed the death zone into, an admittedly bumpy, grassland in just a few months.

Of course there were a few conspiracy theorists who smelt a rat, but they were few, had no resources, were pretty busy trying to simply survive, and when their back up generators ran out of gas and the electricity was turned off, they were in the dark for good.

By the year 2230, eight years after the 'Day of the Dead' things were on the up!

The flood of suicides God had visited upon the Earth had cleared it of a lot of the shit.

The planet was damaged but industry had stopped overnight and the planet was bouncing back. Nature is far more resilient than anyone had really thought. I mean it coped pretty well for the first five billion years, with all those big meteor showers, cosmic rays and celestial whatnots going on.

It's 2322 now. Emperor Alexandra has been dead for 27 years, but her grand daughter Alexandra III is now Emperor for life. She's very popular and has bought many changes including the Tree law.

Everyone has to plant one tree every month. That is 18 Billion trees a year over the old ruins. You can feel the air changing.

Anyone who does not do this is fined one months pay. No matter who they are, how much they earn, or what they do – if they don't plant a tree it's a months pay deducted or fined.

Laws are strict: the Death Penalty applies for any individual who breaks the 'life code' but very few people do. And to be honest, with the world the way it is, when someone does break the 'life code' we are usually better off without them.

All drugs are legal but difficult to get, as is home brewed alcohol, but everyone must work. Physical, mental, childcare, even creating stories, music and entertainment, there is always something someone can do.

If you can't work you are 'returned'. Once you are 'returned' that's it. No more tree planting.

Money had been replaced with a chip – so black markets cannot exist.

The chip is just behind the skin on your left thumb. It requires very little power and runs on crystal electricity. A lot of things now run on solar power, water and even rain power – which no one had thought of before but works really well.

Life is OK. It's a long way from Paradise or even Eden, but it's far better than when I was a boy. Life expectancy is on the up and the air feels cleaner. The Rain doesn't sting any more and last year I went fishing and caught a pure strain fish that wasn't mutated! It tasted a bit muddy but no one was sick which was nice.

We are not really sure what will happen in the future – but it does feel positive and I really hope that yesterday never comes back.

However I've got a bit of a dilemma.

I was one of the lucky ones – I knew someone who knew someone in the Alexandra III Godverment (they thought God-Government was too much of a mouthful) and they put me to work sorting through tonnes of information, on their make shift computers – to see if we could get more people working on the epic clean ups.

A lot of the survivors had set up their own little almost feudal villages, and the Godverment left them alone, but those that had come together in the ruined powerless cities wanted to set up a new world order and it was the job of people like me to help these grow and remain on course for a brighter future.

And I found something. Something not good. Something that I know will get me executed if I ever tell anyone.

So I'm writing this down. Maybe as security but I'm not really sure why. I think in a very sad and strange way it was the right thing to do.

It was a government trick. As many had suspected. It was originally set up by the British, the masters of colonial and imperialistic failure, and they wanted to rule again. It took 37 years of planning. But they did it and they got it right.

Huge clouds of hallucinogenic gas complete with Radio and TV transmissions from drone aircraft and long dead satellites re-animated to spread the word of God. The gas was like an LSD Acid trip and made the people open to suggestion, they saw the faces on the paintings speak to them, because, well, they really wanted to believe.

There was also a file on the hit squads who went round looking for dissidents, un-believers and people who had not seen the broadcast, or not been affected by the gas, and were immediately executed on the spot. Amid all the millions of suicides and deaths a cover-up operation was hardly required.

I've deleted most of the evidence, because, who would I show it to and who would believe me? And most importantly what would I gain? I have a wife now, and two pretty OK children, Sally has a slight mutation, but as long as she wears the hat no-one will mind.

I'm finishing now, as my shift is over and the electricity will be turned off soon. I'm going to print it all out, and seal it in a container behind my bedroom wall. I'll know it's there until I die, and then after that… maybe I'll tell my wife. Not after I die, tell her before I die. Hopefully. Or maybe not.

I think it's best if this piece of history is consigned to history. It was awful and bad and despicable, but they saved the human race…

But will someone have to do this all over again in 2222 years?

The End.

Barnaby and the Berbalang

A short story for short people.

Chapter One:

The Tall House

Barnaby lived in a very tall house.

It was a very tall house indeed.

Very, very, *very*, VERY, **VERY** tall.

So tall, in fact, that often when Barnaby went all the way to the top, his mother couldn't be bothered to come and find him, because it was such a long way to go!

Of course when Barnaby went all the way to the top of the house he often bought a small picnic wrapped up in a big red spotted hankie.

He would bring some nice crusty bread and a small pot of bumberry jam. If he was lucky he'd pinch a small bottle of bumberry juice from the cold room.

What his mother didn't know and I'm sure she would be horrified if she did, was that the tallest room in the tall house was not tall enough for Barnaby who was the small king of a tall world.

He liked to climb out of the WINDOW, which you must never do at home, and sit on the roof of the tall room. It was a very flat roof with a spiky edge, and once upon a time, which should really go at the beginning of the story, but once upon a time it was none the less, once upon a time Barnaby had dragged a small chair all the way up the tall house so that the small king could sit on his tall house on his small chair and survey the large world.

And it was a large world that Barnaby could see from his tall house.

He could see for miles.

And sometimes, on a clear day, he could see five!

Chapter two:

A room with a View.

From his look out point Barnaby could see all.

He could see the three churches of the village, the shop, the train station where his dad went to every morning and came back every evening. He could see the airfield where the great airships were docked and he could see the sea in the distance glinting like a very small silver coin.

Barnaby wished he had a lot more silver coins than he had. He didn't actually have any at all, but he knew that if he had a lot he could buy a motor car and drive off and see the sea.

His mum had told him that the sea was the most amazing thing to see and how that it went on for ever and ever and possibly more. Maybe even to the edge of the world.

His dad said that it was alright if you liked that sort of thing.

Barnaby thought that he probably would like that sort of thing a great deal.

He asked his dad if the sea had an edge and what it was like.

His dad said he wasn't sure.

His mum said that sometimes when the sea met the land it was all sandy, sometimes it was rocky and sometimes it was in between with thousands and thousands of little tiny pebbles.

Barnaby thought hard about this and decided that he'd probably like the rocks best, because there would be caves and things lived in caves…

Chapter Three:

The things in the Tall House.

Now you may think that in the tall house there lived Barnaby, his mum and Barnaby's Dad and you would be right because they are the only people that I have told you about so far.

But!

There were more things living in the tall house, and notice when I say things and not people.

Barnaby had several pets.

He had a pet snail which he kept in a large jar under his windowsill in his bedroom which was half way up the house.

He had wanted to have his bedroom at the top of the tall house, but his mum said she couldn't be bothered to go up all the stairs every time she had to drag him out of bed for school!

So he settled on a room in the middle of the house.

One of the other reasons that Barnaby settled on a room in the middle of the house is that he found he had a lot of trouble with bad dreams. He would wake up in the middle of the night feeling that he was surrounded by darkness. As though evil things were smothering him and corrupting his sleep.

His mother said that if he was in the middle of the house that she and Barnaby's dad could listen out for him in case he had a Nightmare, but of course they never did.

He often wondered why his mum and dad lived in such a tall house when they never went up to the uppest bits and his dad just said that it was left to him by a distant uncle who liked to look at the stars and they should be happy to live in such a distinctive building!

Barnaby couldn't agree more.

Barnaby's snail, which didn't have a name, but was known as Barnaby's snail agreed.

It was happy in the jar, eating all the bumberry jam stalks that Barnaby fed it and occasionally when in season, a pufferclock leaf.

Barnaby's second pet was a gog which he kept in another jar on a shelf in the corner, because gogs like the dark.

Barnaby had also failed to name the gog, so it was also called Barnaby's gog. The snail didn't seem to mind sharing a room with a gog and the gog generally kept itself to itself.

The gog wasn't too keen on Bumberry jam stalks so Barnaby fed it on the ants that trooped across his window sill and off down the side of the house and into his mother's kitchen.

The gog would have about three ants in one go as it was a small gog and not a greedy gog.

At the top of the house near where Barnaby had placed his small chair was a nest and in that nest was a bird. Or sometimes even a family of birds.

The nest was just out of reach for Barnaby, even when he went and got a stick. He waved it around in a sort of half bored way and after throwing it at the nest once he almost lost his balance and toppled off the top of this tall building he was perched upon.

Barnaby decided that watching the birds was probably the safest option and he wasn't that bothered about actually touching them after all.

Chapter Four:

Barnaby's Dad

Now, the dad that Barnaby had was a bad dad.

That is not to say that Barnaby's Dad was BAD, but that the dad he had was bad at being a dad.

Which was sad.

He'd forget Barnaby's birthdays and forget to come to school on special days and once he even forgot Barnaby's name! Which was unforgivable as his wife, Barnaby's mother, often pointed out.

Even though Barnaby's dad was a bad dad, he didn't mean to be bad, it was just that like so many important things in this life, no one had told Barnaby's dad *how* to be a dad and what it was that a good dad did!

For you see, Barnaby's dad didn't have his own dad, so what a dad did he had had to learn by simple guess work, and the odd discrete word with one of his fellow dads who worked with him in the Big Town.

One of the dads who worked with Barnaby's dad in the Big Town, one day told Barnaby's dad that being a dad was all about listening. Listening to what your children wanted and what they liked to do and what they were scared of and how you, as their Dad, could make their world a better and safer place for them to be.

Barnaby's Dad thought this sounded like good advice. He resolved to have a chat with his son and listen to what it was that he had to say.

However, when Barnaby's Dad got home, he found that Barnaby was in his usual place at the top of the house, he had waved to him from the pavement outside, and unfortunately Barnaby's Dad had bonked his knee at work and it just hurt too much for him to climb all those stairs.

He resolved to remember to talk and listen to Barnaby when he came down stairs for tea. But by the time young Barnaby came down his Dad had read the newspaper and forgotten all about listening to what his son would say.

So, like so many other tea times, they sat and sipped their tea and munched on their bumberry jam cakes whilst listening to the wireless news of goings on in foreign lands.

Not a word was said.

Except by Barnaby's mother who asked him if he had enough when he finished his cake.

Barnaby nodded.

So Barnaby's lack of good dad-ness was another thing that drove him up the many stairs into the topmost room of their terribly tall house.

Taller in fact than any of the tall houses in Tall House Street and taller, even, than the Keep on the Borderlands, which was widely regarded as a very tall keep indeed.

"Wow!" People would say, that's one tall house!

And they would wave at the tiny boy perched on the top of the topmost roof waving back at them.

Chapter Five:

A touch like ice cubes.

You may have thought that I had told you all about all of the beings who lived in the house, for have I not told you of Barnaby, his mother, his Dad, Barnaby's snail and Barnaby's gog?

Yes I have!

But then again I have not. For there was a further being in the house and one who was not a family member, and did not live in a jar in Barnaby's room.

For in the house at the top under the floorboards and inside the hollow walls.

Awake after sunset and asleep at sunrise was an inky black creature.

A creature of the night.

A creature with a black heart.

A creature with black eyes.

A creature with a toothy grin.

A creature that had been watching Barnaby for a long time and secretly whispering in his ear as he slept.

Leaning silently out of the gaps between the ceiling and the floorboards and breathing into Barnaby's small ears. Whispering. Gibbering. Cackling.

Sometimes even touching Barnaby's fresh white skin with a touch so soft it felt to Barnaby that he was being caressed by moonbeams as he slept.

He would awake to feel a coldness on his cheek as though a dry ice cube had been placed there.

He would shiver, draw his three blankets about him and then drift off once more to a light sleep. He wouldn't even notice the creature poised inched above his head. Hiding in the shadows still as a vault. Hardly daring to breathe less its breath should awake the dozing boy.

As Barnaby shuffled back to the land of Nod the BERBALANG would grin and chuckle to itself, and climb back through the gaps in the walls into its night time pitch black world.

Chapter Six:

The Berbalang

Yes! A Berbalang!

What is a Berbalang? I know is the question you want to ask.

Well.

That is a very good question.

Barnaby's Berbalang is one of the only ones I have heard of, but I am sure there must be more.

Maybe you have lain awake at night listening to the sound of some unidentified scratching in the walls?

Or a skitter under the floor boards?

Or even the faint brush of a cobweb across your sleeping face?

Your mother probably told you that it was mice and not to worry. But I'd wager that it was a Berbalang. Waiting and listening for your mummy to leave the room and for you to go to sleep for it to poke out its scaly dark head and breathe words into your receptive, defenseless ears.

For a Berbalang lives and feeds on nightmares. And much like we grow crops in the fields, the Berbalang has to nurture and cultivate the bad dreams into such nightmares of terror and complexity that they are like a five course meal, with ice cream to finish!

The Berbalang is a solitary being with leathery wings, is spends the great deal of its time in hibernation much like a hedge-hog! But when it wakes up it has a terrible hunger in its scaly belly and knows the hunger will only be sated by the most repellent and ugly dream!

A bad dream is just not good enough for a Berbalang, it needs a NIGHTMARE.

And at five past midnight on this particular night the Berbalang hooked its gnarled tail around a beam in the attic and gently slipped through a gap in the boards and lowered itself inches above Barnaby's face, slowly drifting in the cool midnight air floating in from Barnaby's open window.

As the Berbalang floated above Barnaby it began to whisper horrid words and evil thoughts which found their way into poor Barnaby's ears.

He'd shifted and a frown passed over his face, as if an unpleasant thought had passed through his mind, which was indeed what had happened!

The Berbalang, hanging from his tail over Barnaby's face, gibbered to itself in delight as it felt the first forming of Barnaby's nightmare, like the smell of a beautiful feast drifting from a kitchen to your hungry nose.

A tiny taste of the sensory delights to come.

The Berbalang, now more excited lowered itself to within licking distance of Barnaby's ear and whispered anew.

Such words and deeds that I cannot repeat here in case your mummy found this book and was so horrified at the words contained here in, that she would throw the book away and you would never know how the story ended!

The Berbalang began to feed on the sumptuous nightmares it had cooked up inside Barnaby's little head. It licked its lips and rubbed its rotten hands.

Chapter Seven:

Suddenly!

Suddenly, something happened that the Berbalang had not foreseen, being so entranced at the intoxicating flavour of this vicious dream it was sipping, it was caught completely off guard!

The door to Barnaby's room swung open and with a click the room was filled with light!

Stepping into Barnaby's room was Barnaby's bad at being a dad Dad, with a cup of warm milk in his hand.

The poor terrified Berbalang didn't know what to do, but within a second has melded itself against a shadow on the wall and stuck there, silent as the dead.

Barnaby shifted in the light and his face relaxed as the nightmare cooked up by the Berbalang began to dissipate and fade away.

Barnaby's dad sat down on the chair next to Barnaby. I think he was relieved that Barnaby was asleep and that he didn't have to actually talk with his son, as his wife had told him to do.

He sat by Barnaby's bed for a while and told Barnaby how much he loved him, which is always easiest to do when the other person isn't listening!

After a while Barnaby's Dad stopped. And thinking Barnaby to be still asleep kissed him lightly on the forehead and made to leave the room.

"I love you too Dad," said Barnaby. Who had been awake from the moment his dad had walked into the room.

"Thanks son," said Barnaby's Dad stopping on his way to the door. "Would you like me to help you paint the roof at the weekend?"

"Oh yes please that would be brilliant!" said Barnaby.

"Good. We'll do that. Sweet dreams son."

"Sweet dreams dad."

Barnaby's dad smiled and left the room, closing the door with a soft click and leaving the warm milk on the chair beside Barnaby's bed.

Barnaby smiled and reached for the light switch.

But something in his head told him to stop.

Look around.

Something was not quite right.

Barnaby had lived in his room for hundreds and hundreds of days and hundred and hundreds of nights and he knew what his room looked like. Barnaby's Dad who never came to Barnaby's room, wouldn't have noticed if Barnaby had painted the room Green and grown bumberry plants from his sock drawer.

But Barnaby, who was a very observant boy could see that something was different.

Very slowly indeed, Barnaby pretended to yawn and stretch his arms and then with a speed of an arrow, he plunged his hand into the inky black darkness by the curtain and grabbed the shadow he saw hiding there.

There was a gasp and Barnaby felt his hand grasp something cold and gnarled. The thing zoomed up the wall pulling Barnaby with him, but the boy would not let go. He was a brave boy, having scaled the Tor at Enon, by himself and he had stood up to Marcus Flinch the School Bully many times, but this was real courage.

Barnaby pulled and yanked and brought the Berbalang out into the light of the room where he gaped at the ugliness of the writhing creature that cackled and hissed as it tried to break free from the boy's grip.

Chapter Eight:

What would you say to a Berbalang?

Barnaby knew that his grip wasn't going to last long, so using all his might he shoved the Berbalang into his toy chest at the foot of his bed and slammed down the lid, sitting on it as he did so.

The Berbalang bashed about for a moment then was still.

Barnaby thought for a moment. Then spoke.

"What are you doing in my room?" He asked quite reasonably considering the circumstances.

There was a grizzly cough like sound from the toy chest.

"What are you doing in my room!" Barnaby asked again this time a little more loudly and a little more strongly.

"I was eating your nightmares…" whispered the Berbalang in its throaty hissing voice.

Barnaby was quite surprised by the answer. He hadn't really expected the thing to speak at all, least of all be told that it had been feeding on his nocturnal thought!

"Eating my nightmares?"

"Yesss… Very nice they were too. Yum. Yum."

"Why do you have to eat my nightmares?"

"Because they are tasty, stupid boy!"

"Do you make me have the bad dreams?" Asked Barnaby who was by no means a stupid boy.

"Yes I feed you the nightmares and you feed me! Yum Yum!"

"That's horrible!" Said Barnaby who was right.

"Not horrible yum yum!"

"Why does it have to be Bad dreams, why cant you eat nice dreams?"

"Berbalang like Nasty dreams! Yes!"

Berbalang? Barnaby said to himself. So that's what you are.

"Well. Good night Berbalang!" I'm going to sleep now and have some nice dreams.

Barnaby carefully locked the toy chest and then tied a long length of string around the chest several times and then tied a big sheet around the chest, then he heaved the chest to the window sill and tied the chest there, just sitting, ready to fall all the way to the street below.

He could hear the Berbalang cursing and scratching as he fiddled with the chest, but Barnaby ignored it.

Eventually satisfied that his work was done for the time being, Barnaby climbed back in to Bed, he drank the mug of milk, which was cold now and wiping the milk moustache from his face he settled back into his soft pillow and slipped in to the land of nod. Where he was visited by absolutely super dreams all night, not a hint of nasty stuff at all.

Chapter nine:

In the morning.

The following Day Barnaby got ready for school like any other day and after wishing the Berbalang good-bye headed off down stairs to have his usual Bumberry jam on toast with dandelion tea.

His mother was surprised to see him so awake and bright eyed, but when Barnaby told her that he had slept well and hadn't been visited by the nightmares, she smiled to herself and felt happy that her little boy was growing up and out growing his bad dreams.

After Barnaby had left the house for school, she phoned Barnaby's Dad at work and told him that Barnaby hadn't had bad dreams that night and Barnaby's Dad felt good, because he felt that because he had had his little chat with his son, he had made everything alright.

Meanwhile the Berbalang scratched and picked at the seams in the wood in the toy box. Cursing and seething to itself.

Barnaby's day at school was much the same as the other several billion days of school he had had to endure over the countless years he had been there. At lunch time he was going to tell his best friend Millicent about the Berbalang, but as she was a girl, he thought she might be scared. So he didn't.

At the end of his science class that afternoon, Barnaby stayed behind and asked his teacher a few questions.

His teacher replied that he had never heard of a Berbalang, maybe Barnaby should ask the History teacher if it was a creature of legend or maybe the English master if it was from a book?

However, the science teacher did lend Barnaby a book, which made Barnaby very pleased indeed.

Chapter Ten:

The Book.

"Hey Berbalang," said Barnaby as he climbed onto the Toy chest as it teetered on the windowsill.

"Let me out." Hissed the Berbalang.

"Maybe I will and maybe….I won't. I think we need to make a deal here."

"No deal. Berbalang does what they want to."

"Oh well maybe I will just push you out of the window then." Barnaby pushed the box a little further out over the ledge, he could hear all the toys inside slide forward.

"No!" choked the thing.

"Want to make a deal?"

"What you want?" Said the Berbalang, a definite trace of fear in its voice.

"Well, why do you have to eat Nightmares? Have you ever tried eating a nice dream?"

"No! Berbalang eat nasty dreams, always have, always will!"

"Well that *is* a shame. You'll just have to stay in the box then."

The Berbalang said some very rude words some of which Barnaby knew and some he thought he would have to ask Millicent, who although a girl, knew a vast array of expletives and things that would shock even someone who thought they knew a thing or two about swearing.

"Well if you promise to just leave me alone then I will let you out."

"?" Said the Berbalang.

"Well, my mum told me it was cruel to keep things caged up." Said Barnaby looking at his pet snail and his pet gog.

"Yes, you should let me out, very cruel to keep me caged like this. Coff, coff." Coughed the Berbalang.

"Ok then, I'll let you out, I'm going to open the lid now and you can just climb away, OK?"

"Er… OK!"

"And you promise to leave me alone?"

"Yes, no more Yum Yum from you! He he he."

Barnaby had undone the string and the sheet and slowly opened the lid of the chest.

The Berbalang sprang out like a hideous malformed Jack-in-the-box, but Barnaby was ready for it and bashed it across the head in a superb blow with the huge hard backed book the Science Teacher had lent him.

The Berbalang crashed to the floor, where Barnaby sat on him.

Then taking the string, he began to tie up the Berbalang using the knots he had learned from the book, which was the Big Book of Knots!

After a short while, the Berbalang was all tied up, Barnaby pulled the creature over to his bed and tied it to the headboard of his bed.

He put a little gag in the Berbalang mouth using his red spotted hankie.

When the Berbalang finally woke up, it writhed and kicked against the string tying it all up but to no avail.

The knots Barnaby had learnt from the big book of knots were just too knotty!

“Now, we are going to have a little experiment and see if you can make do on nice dreams Berbalang, what do you think?” Barnaby pulled down the red spotted hankie then quickly shoved it back in the Berbalang's mouths after the tirade of rude words that spew forth.

“That was predictable,” said Barnaby, climbing into bed. “I do hope to have some nice dreams tonight.” said Barnaby, “why don’t you give it a go, they might taste ok?”

So Barnaby turned out the light and went off to sleep.

Chapter Eleven:

Bad Dreams.

The first few night with the Berbalang were not completely nightmare free. But they certainly weren't the nasty nights that Barnaby had been used to.

After about half a week, the Berbalang, began to relent. He was uncomfortable, and although Barnaby had loosened a lot of the knots and had even fed the Berbalang on some nasty thoughts, the Berbalang could see that Barnaby was made of stern stuff and was not going to let him go.

So the Berbalang tried a nice dream. It truly hurt the Berbalang to talk of holidays and hot air balloons and mountains of snow. Pretty girls, loads of toys and chests of treasure. But something strange happened, the Berbalang found that these dreams tasted sweet. It was like having pudding, without having dinner first.

This isn't all bad thought the Berbalang.

The next day Barnaby woke up and spoke to his Captured Creature. "Thank you for my nice dreams last night. They were really great, they can't have been too bad can they?"

"Humph." Humphed the Berbalang.

"Well, look Berbalang, do you really like living in the grubby attic? Where it is cold and dark and smells of damp wood?"

"Humph." Humphed the Berbalang again.

"If you just feed me one nice dream a night, you can have a bed in this room and I'll bring you things if you want them, a pillow, a blanket, whatever you would like.

"Humph." Humphed the Berbalang, though this humph, was defiantly less humphie than the previous humph!

So Barnaby went and emptied out the toy chest and filled it with blankets and pillows, he put a lamp in the corner which cast a big shadow, and he placed the chest in the shadow. Then he put the

Berbalang in the chest and undid the last few knots, keeping an eye on the Big Book Of Knots which was still within easy reach.

The Berbalang tested the bedding as it rubbed its wrists.

"Never had a bed." Said the Berbalang.

"What else do you want?"

"Never had a cup of milk."

"I'll get you one."

"Never had a blanket, or a pillow or a… or a… or a…"

"What?"

"Never had a friend." Said the Berbalang.

"Well, we know how to change all of those things don't we?"

Barnaby put out his small hand and held it in front of the small scaly creature that had given him nightmares for so long.

"Shake?" he said.

The Berbalang hesitated then put his gnarled clawed hand into Barnaby's and shook with enthusiasm.

After that Barnaby's mother was amazed at the change in her son, which she put down to Barnaby's dad having talked to him.

Barnaby would come down the stairs bright eyes and smiling, having had a night of restful sleep.

Barnaby's Dad was happy as he felt that his quick chat had made all the world of difference and when they did go up and paint the roof, he found that he really enjoyed hanging out with his son and that the top of the tall house was actually a really cool place to be!

The Berbalang was happy too as he had a nice bed, milk to drink, the run of the house at night time and whenever he felt the need for something savoury he'd just whisper a short Nasty dream into Barnaby's ear at the beginning of the evening then cover all traces with a lengthy good dream which seem to suit everyone.

And as a reward for Barnaby being so good, his dad took him for a day trip to the seaside where Barnaby was able to explore all the rock pools, beaches and caves.

He even bought an interesting shaped rock back for the Berbalang, to file his claws on. The Berbalang was delighted. He'd never had a present before.

That night Barnaby had wonderful dreams all of his own.

The End

THE SLEEPY WORLD OF BALTHAZAR

The naughtiest boy who ever lived, ever!

This is a children's book for children, written by me, a grown up child.

This is ***not*** for people who don't find childish things funny!

A very naughty little boy indeed.

Once upon a time, a long time from now, a long way away on an island not like our own. There lived a little boy.

Balthazar was his name and naughtiness was his game! He'd pick bogies and wipe them on other kid's cheeks. He'd steal their pencils and hide them for weeks,

He'd steal nice cakes from their pack lunches, he'd hide in the corner and take great munches!

He pulled the girl's pony tails and made the little boys eat snails!

So naughty even the Gods noticed.

But the Gods noticed that Balthazar was the naughtiest boy on the island and sent a curse down to tame him.

They made him sleepy. Sleepy as a dog that has run a thousand miles. Balthazar could hardly muster up the strength to flick a bogie, let alone pick his nose for one.

He stopped stealing the chocolate cakes cause he couldn't be bothered to find the lunch boxes.

His teachers thought that he must have decided to be good after all, but really he was just plotting. He knew that one day he would be awake again.

So he made a plan.

The plan.

He thought to himself that he would sleep. And sleep and sleep until he had stored up a whole load of energy so that he could go and be really naughty!

A naughtiness never before seen. A naughtiness that would leave his teachers open mouthed and wide eyed.

Oh yes this naughtiness was going to be… well, Naughty!!!

A short chapter.

It was the long weekend before the yearly hogging and Balthazar felt restless but tired. He went to his room and lay down on his bed. Soon he was asleep. He slept for the rest of the day. His dreams were vivid and long.

A shorter chapter.

When he awoke he was still tired, so he had a glass of water, then went back to sleep and slept another day.

A chapter in which the title of the chapter is longer than the chapter itself.

And another.

The Next (and slightly longer) chapter.

After three days sleep he awoke with a monster gnawing in his belly.

A chapter in which Balthazar has lunch.

Actually Balthazar had breakfast. Bumberry jam and crusty bread, which was his favourite. With a gallon of sweet tea.

He was well happy after that. And more importantly he was awake! His mind swam with naughty thoughts.

Balthazar gets down to serious naughtiness.

When he finally arrived at school, Balthazar deliberately waited outside the school gates until he was 13 minutes late, and still he didn't feel tired. He could feel his energy and awakeness bubbling up inside himself.

He was so full of energy he skipped into the classroom, and trod on the toes of Pippie Moonsock and made her cry. Without stopping for a moment, he did a little pirouette and smashed the see-through vase on the lower window sill with a flick of his coat tails, sending Miss Plinkitons collection of Purplebells sailing across the floor.

The tinkling of broken glass was like a symphony to naughty Balthazar's ears.

Without pausing to survey the scene, he snatched a pen from Percy's hand and drew a big squiggle along the wall as he ran to the pile of cushions by the blue sand pit.

As he ran he delved deep into his own nostril with his grubby pointing finger, (or bottom wiping finger as Balthazar liked to call it), and produced the freshest gloopyiest biggest, greenest, stickiest, bogie that there ever has been. Ever.

With a skill that an Olympic archer would be jealous off, Balthazar flicked the bogie which sailed through the air in a beautiful arch and landed in the open mouth of Muttigule Whimp the boy with the curly hair.

Muttigule was so shocked that he gulped and swallowed the enormous bogie!

There was a pause as the whole class stared open mouthed as they saw the lump in Muttigules throat pass down his neck and into his tummy.

Balthazar shrieked with delight and jumped into the air!

His act of naughtiness was the best ever!

Muttigule Whimp whimpered and looked pleadingly around, then he roared! It looked like he turned inside out as his whole tummy contents threw forth from his mouth and showered the kids from head to toe in bogie sick mix!

Balthazar was so excited that he did a little dance and jumped onto a chair, just like Fred Astair!

The noise of the screaming kids wallowing in sick bogie mix was so loud that it floated up to one of the lower clouds where one of the Gods, who was having a bit of a quiet day-off, heard it.

He peered over the side of his cloud and with his magic God-eyes, looked down to see what all the palaver was about.

When he saw what had been going on he had to admit to being quite impressed. Never before in all his years of Godding had he ever seen such a massive amount of naughtiness in such a small amount of time. However Balthazar had clearly been very naughty and had to be punished.

The little God took out his God phone and phoned the big God.

Back with Balthazar.

Balthazar was standing in the middle of a large circular carpet, in the middle of a large room.

Two large people were standing by a large desk talking to a small man, who had a large storm cloud floating above his small wig.

Balthazar had a large smile on his small face and a large feeling of success inside his small body. He could hardly stand still he was so proud and full of himself.

He knew that there was nothing the adults could do to him that would take away from his status of naughtiest boy ever.

The small man with the small wig and the large thunder cloud. Stood up and advanced upon the small Balthazar.

Looking Down from a cloud.

The little God on the cloud used his God eyes to look through the roof of the building and see what was happening with naughty Balthazar.

He rested his elbows on the comfy cloud and peered over the edge. His long beard kept blowing into his face, but once he had tucked it away he could really concentrate.

The little God, let out a little titter, something was about to happen, he could feel it, as little sparks of blue lightning began to appear below him. He was so excited he could hardly contain himself and he started to fidget.

Balthazar the naughtiest boy in the world.

Balthazar may have been the naughtiest boy in the world, but he still wasn't finished yet.

He stood there in the middle of the circular carpet listening to the Head Teacher telling him what a naughty boy he was, which to Balthazar was like receiving an Oscar. He was smiling from ear to ear.

Suddenly Balthazar realised that the room had gone quiet, he could see that the teacher had finished telling him off and was waiting for him to say something.

Balthazar thought for a moment and looked right into the eyes of the Head Teacher, and he looked beyond the eyes of the teacher and looked into the very soul of that teacher and then do you know what Balthazar said?

Do you?

Well you are wrong, because he didn't say anything, he just did a big fart!

All that bumberry jam he had had for breakfast had been eaten for a reason!

It was the loudest, noisiest, stinkiest fart in the history of the world. It started as a loud CLAP and rose higher in pitch until it was just a SQUEAK that seemed to last an incredibly long time, and ended up with a final QUACK that sounded like a duck had just appeared in the room, and made the windows rattle.

Wasn't that the naughtiest thing Balthazar could have done?

The green gas from Balthazar's bottom rose in to the air as the head teacher went redder and redder, Balthazar was delighted to hear that the two teachers both giggled to each other.

Balthazar smiled broadly. He had completed his mission, and he basked in the rage of his head teacher, as one would bask in the rays of the sun.

And then.

Kazoooooooom!

There was an incredible flash of light and Balthazar was no more.

In the middle of the circular carpet was a little pair of shoes with little wafts of smoke drifting from them.

From the little god's view point, it was almost exactly like looking down on a huge dart board.

The little God could hardly contain himself he was so excited, he quickly pulled his God phone from his robes dialled a quick number and spoke into the phone.

"Oh good shot your Holiness, very, very good."

Heaven or Hell?

Balthazar blinked, and looked around, his feeling of happiness slipped away as his eyes took in his environment.

Sitting in front of him on a huge throne made of thousands of little skulls was a huge God. Something told Balthazar that he wasn't in Kansas anymore.

Something also told Balthazar that Neitche was probably right: This God didn't look very good at all.

Balthazar looked at his hands - he was covered in soot and his clothes were all black and burnt, his hair was like a battlefield. He realised that he wasn't smiling and that his feeling of happiness had completely gone.

Balthazar realised that the God was speaking to him, but he could hear the words in his head, the God was talking into his mind!

The God said that there was a need for people as naughty as Balthazar and that he was too naughty to be on earth, and that the God was going to send him somewhere to work for a 100 years.

Balthazar felt quite worried.

He didn't like the sound of this.

The God clapped his God sized hands and Balthazar reappeared in one of the most revolting places in the universe.

The God had sent Balthazar to work for 100 years in the stickiest Bogie mines! He would spend a century magic-ing bogies from the mines into peoples noses.

Oh well, thought Balthazar, could have been worse, I could have been sent to work in the Fart swamps!

The End

What they say about The Sleepy World of Balthazar:

How many percent did I like it? 92.5%

Arujuna aged 9

I liked the story because it has funny words, and has very short chapters.

Ricki Aged 9

That book is wicked, there is nothing to change, I will buy it when it comes out.

Dominic Aged 9

Balthazar is a real nutcase!

Gurpreet Aged 9

I liked the book because it was hilarious, a bit sick and wonderful.

Nivi Aged 9

The description was described well.

Esra Aged 9.

It was so funny I couldn't stop laughing! I think you are a good story writer.

Anoth Aged 9

I know what you mean by Bogey Sick mix!!!! Because I have very dirty slime indeed!

Zac and Jack Aged 10

I didn't like your book because it was disgusting and he was not doing the right thing.

Sarah Aged 9

If they don't get this published they are missing out on a lot and this story will be loved by children especially.

Raveena Aged 9

GOOD VIBRATIONS

A LONGER SHORT STORY

Chapter 1

Your aura before ya!

Frond had never felt that she had fitted in with the rest of the class.

It wasn't that she was a freak, a mutant or a weirdo, or even that she was ginger, fat or particularly stupid.

She just didn't fit in.

She couldn't work it out, and I don't really think that anyone really cared to spend that much time in her company to bother to find out.

What was wrong with her?

Well, she did have a stupid name, but she had Hippy parents, and besides lots of famous people have stupid names and people still like them. Look at Sting, or Bono or Cher she thought to herself or even Madonna or Lulu for heavens sake. No it wasn't Frond.

She wasn't even an unattractive girl, in fact, for those that did spend some time with her, maybe someone forced to sit next to her on the bus, or in class, when all the other chairs were taken, they may have noticed her potential classic curves, her leadership countenance and her athletic build.

Her blues eyes sparkled and her soul was filled with love and light.

Her aura, however, was crap.

People just couldn't get on with her. I tried and I know what is wrong with her, but I still couldn't get on with the girl.

Her parents, Mr. and Mrs. Hazzah, worried that she was spending too much time on her own, but secretly not blaming anyone, sent her to this specialist and that psychoanalyst, but to no avail.

Nobody, but nobody could find anything actually wrong with Frond, she just didn't *fit in.*

"Curses!" Cried her father, Derek Hazzah, a ladies shoe designer on £30,000 a year, "We've," he continued," been cursed with a scientific enigma for a child!"

"Alas and alak!" screeched Imelda Hazzah, Frond's Mum and Derek's wife, a lady who lunched and helped out at the local school for deaf children, "why couldn't Frond have had a decent ailment, like the children at the school I help out at!?"

Frond's mother collapsed sobbing into the arms of Derek, having just returned from another meeting with some psychoanalyst, or was it a psychologist? I forget which it was. I don't think she actually told me. It certainly isn't important.

"If Frond was deaf, at least the other mothers would feel sorry for me and not look at me like I was a plague bearer, like they do!" Wailed Imelda.

Frond, sitting on the third step up in the hallway listened with interest. The she went to her room.

Sitting on her bed underneath a huge map of the world, Frond wondered if there were others in the world that had the same effect on others that she did. Was there perhaps, a commune somewhere, where everyone knew that they weren't going to get along, so didn't bother and just put up with the fact that they wouldn't like each other?

Or perhaps an island in the Pacific, where no-one spoke to each other and just met on alternate Thursdays to buy food and swap CD's.

Unlikely thought Frond, and even if there was, how would she get the money to get there? Mum and Dad didn't have any, so there wasn't even any money to steal if she knew where the money to steal, which wasn't there, was if you take my meaning.

Bugger, thought Frond, why did I have to have skint Hippy parents? And turning out the light she went to sleep.

Chapter 2

Twelve million miles a minute.

The next day and sometime later, whilst being generally ignored and looked at through the corner of eyes by the other school kinds, Frond got bored.

She had already walked around the playing field seven times and she still had twenty eight minutes before afternoon Math's.

'It's the library for me,' thought Frond as she espied fast approaching grey clouds.

Having quite a lot of time to herself, as children with no friends often do, Frond knew her way around the library pretty well. She knew where all the cool books with the big pictures were, she knew the best place to read without being disturbed and most importantly she knew the place where the books with the pictures of naked people were. This is where she made a bee line for.

As she strolled down the crappily-lino-d floors between the aching shelves and her blazered would-be chums, Frond noticed a strange thing.

At the corner of geometry and Gardening, there was in the ceiling a 'T' shape of neon strip lighting tubes. One of the tubes was beaming away sending out millions of light particles per second and showering the shelves and upturned faces with glorious light.

The other, however, was not. From its cylindrical body reeked an evil, vicious green light, the colour of light that seeped under the door to the room where the swamp thing lives. The sort of light that actually makes you feel ill and is the colour of your deepest gut wrenching spew, after drinking Southern Comfort and absinthe.

Its evil light came out in fits and starts like an epileptic sun, flickering on and off, like a disco strobe. This sickly light trickled over the shelves and eventually got to the floor where it was eaten up by the hungry light absorbing grey lino.

What Frond noticed was this: She had only one shadow. That's all very well, I hear you cry, there are two lights but one is crap! QED Two lights, one shadow.

Not so! Say I! Two constant shadows, yes, if both tubes of illumination were constantly pumping of life giving light, but no! There should be one constant shadow from the constant lamp and one mutant feeble undernourished shadow winking on and off.

Surely then, two shadows, one constant and one flickering and dull like a politicians smile.

But no, they were not. The sickly lamps fits and coughs like a choking tramp, produced no shadow of Frond at all.

Frond peered closer. Emanating from her feet was one shadow. She peered at some length and then she peered some more. Then she peered at the two strip lights, holding her hands against the flying particles rushing through the sky into her eyes.

'Crikey!' said Frond, as perhaps you might.

'That's odd,' she offered by way of an astute observation.

Stepping off into the area of light illuminated by another bulb, Frond examined her shadow, and found that as she had expected there it was. One constant shadow.

Returning to the flicker stick, she squinted into the light and then squinted away the sun dogs in her eyes, until she could make out the shadow on the floor.

Realising that she now only had ten minutes to get to registration before afternoon Maths, Frond left the increasingly interesting library and headed off to room 5:23.

Chapter 3

Masterful Movements.

Four minutes later, Frond found herself walking along a busy corridor, surrounded by her human exclusion zone that surrounded her wherever she went.

People didn't like to get too close to her, so she could walk straight through crowds like a knife through custard. Striding into view she espied Mr. Erik, the physics teacher.

Frond, seeing a possible answer here, decided to risk it:

"Er, Mr. Erik, sir…" Launched Frond. Completely failing to broadside the teacher as he continued to plough through the miasma of shrieking kids.

"MR. ERIK!" Assailed Frond, this time getting his verbal missile to make serious impact.

The good ship Erik, halted in the swirling sea of kids and heaved to.

"Yes?" The voice of power raised above the splat of sound that filled the corridor.

"Er, Mr. Erik, sir, I have found something that I think I would like to show you. As head of Physics. Sir?" Voiced Frond, raising her voice at the end like so many Americans and TV celebrities do, nowadays.

"What is that then, Frond Hazzah?" The good ship Erik was now hard astern, sending white horses of school kids to each side as he powered back along the corridor.

"Erm, it would be easier if I just showed it to you, sir. It's the lighting in the Library, by the Gardening section. It's, er. Well. It's er, weird? Sir." Struggled Frond.

"Weird?" Erik had now anchored, inches away from Frond, something that she didn't encounter very often, what with being so unpleasant to be around and all.

"Weird in what way Frond?" Followed the physics teacher.

"Well, erm, ulp, it's a light, sir, it isn't casting a shadow even when it's er, actually…on?" Winced Frond.

"Light not on, casting shadow?" Eyebrow firmly raised.

"No sir. Light ON, *Not* casting shadow. Sir." Hint of pleading.

"Light on? No shadow?" Hint of interest.

"Yes sir. That is what it is doing sir. Come and see?" Hint of desperation.

"In the library, you say?" Peer, peer.

"Yes. By Gardening." Shrinking.

"Let's have a look at this shadow of yours then, hmmm?" Rising.

"Yes sir. Thank you sir." Relieved.

Being one of the longer conversations that Frond had had with staff she thought that it had gone rather well. She followed in the wake of the good ship Erik as it passed 4B Home Economics, where she had seen Mr. Emsworth the Math's teacher de-flower Sasha Golden the 5th form Lolita. It was amazing what you could notice when people didn't want to see you thought Frond.

Chapter 4

The evidence is evident.

Arriving at the library, Frond led Mr. Erik to the junction of geometry and gardening. Sure enough there was the bright solid shadow and casting tube and there was the nasty, flickering green slime light snot shadow caster.

Frond maneuvered herself to optimum position and pointed at her shadow.

"Look sir!" Quite clearly Frond had one shadow. Whilst all around had two, a strong one and a feeble one. Like most double acts.

"Hmmm." Rumbled Mr. Erik. "Stand aside." Erik moved into Frond's position.

The teacher and the un-loved girl pondered what they saw for a moment before speaking.

"You have got two shadows Mr. Erik sir. I don't. Why is that sir?" Questioned Frond.

"Sir?" Frond tilted her head on one side.

"Sir?" Frond tried the other side.

Expressions of deepest thought crossed Mr. Erik's lined face. He examined the shadows on the floor and peered at the two neon tubes.

"Frond," he said, in a bassy tone, "Frond, I think it must be something to do with reflection and the blazer you are wearing," he said most unconvincingly.

"I don't think so sir, because…"

"Frond, it is ten after three, are you not supposed to be in afternoon registration with Mr. Emsworth?"

"Well, yes sir, but I thought…" Struggled Frond.

"Thank you for pointing out the damaged bulb, Frond, I will see that it gets replaced at once. And I will give you TEN merit points for your vigilance, public thinking and scientific enquiry. Well done." Erik smiled at Frond, and she knew that it was time to make a strategic maneuvre. This was the 'kind offer', she knew if she pushed it she'd probably end up with a detention.

"Thank you sir." And so saying Frond did a smart about turn and headed off to Afternoon registration with Mr. Emsworth, the underage school girl shagger.

Chapter 5

Moving from one place to another place.

That night after Frond's Mum had collected tea from outside Frond's door, where she preferred to leave it, Frond heard the front door bell go. They didn't really get a lot of unexpected callers, so Frond listened in. She was even more surprised to hear the unmistakable sound of Mr. Erik's steam boat voice seep through the unpainted floor boards and up past the Moroccan carpet in her room.

She listened in. Word's like 'frequency' and 'refraction' filtered through and unmistakably, 'away' and 'research'.

Ooops thought Frond, I should have kept my mouth shut.

Ooops was right.

Sure enough a week later, Frond found herself with a small suitcase packed with a weeks worth of clean pants and socks, sitting on the back seat of a taxi heading, she knew not where for she knew not how long.

As the Taxi rounded the corner of her road, obscuring her house, Frond could see her parents and it didn't look like they were crying.

In the 'centre' as the staff like to refer to it, Frond found that she actually had a better quality of life than she had had at home. The food was pretty good, she had a big room with a play station, which she had never had before. She didn't get any nasty jibes from any of the other kids and she could see that a lot of the other kids were in a far worse state than she had ever been in.

Whilst at lunch in the canteen on the third day, just when she was beginning to get the hang of the place and work out where the salad bar was, and which table she should it at, the boy opposite her, who had actually said hello and smiled at her, burst into flame and was consumed before her very eyes.

By the time the canteen staff had put the fire out with big red fire extinguishers, all that was left were the metal braces from his teeth and a belt buckle on his chair.

Nobody spoke for the rest of the day.

Chapter 6

A Doctor calls.

A day after that, Frond had a brain scan, which was actually quite exciting as she got put on a trolley and pushed into the centre of a big machine that looked like a huge white toilet roll.

Once inside, it made all sorts of klonking noises, then she was shown some photographs of the inside of her brain by a very smiley nurse and a very black doctor. He had beautiful smooth skin like mahogany.

They seemed very excited about something and rushed off to speak to other weird looking medical staff.

They left Frond, sitting on the trolley by the big toilet roll. No body ever tells me their name she thought.

Then she wandered off.

Over the next length of indiscernible time Frond was measured, weighed, photographed, exposed to all sorts of lights and colours, x-rayed and gamma-rayed and probably all sorts of totally illegal things that scientists just can't help them-selves from doing.

After what seemed a month or possibly two, the very black doctor with mahogany skin came to Frond's room and sat on her bed.

"Hello Doctor," said Frond, as you would.

"Hello Frond," said the doctor, being reasonably well informed on the ways of conversation.

"How am I Doctor?" Quizzical eyebrows furrowing.

"Well Frond, This is a bit difficult to explain." Mouth dry, thinking hard, "but it appears that you actually exist, er…" Avoiding eye contact, "in, er, in a different time signature to everyone else."

"Wot?"

"Er, well. You see to most people a second is this long…….See, but to you a second is a different length of time. You actually run at a different frequency, and the thing is , you are actually blinking in and out of this dimension constantly, which is why you don't fit in, because you ain't supposed to *be* here."

"Oh, where am I supposed to be then?"

"Good question, a very good question and indeed a question that we have spent a GREAT deal of time thinking about."

"Yes?.."

"Well, you see Frond, Dimension studies are in their infancy, what with a lack of public interest, bad press from silly films, and a lack of government funding. Not to mention all sorts of technical problems like black holes, time slips, complicated stuff like that and to be honest, er, we just don't know."

"Oh."

"But we can GUESS!! And my colleagues and I have a pretty good idea where the dimension that you came from, or at least are supposed to be in, is and also we are fairly confident that we have the technology to make the jump!" Smiling and sitting back in triumph. Arms folded!

"So what you mean is that, I am in the wrong dimension. You know, or think you know how and where this dimension is and you think that you can, er, transport me there? And in this dimension I would be just like a normal girl with friends and people would want to talk to me because I was vibrating at the right speed? Is that it Doc?" Thinking hard.

"Excellent Frond! Well done for grasping it."

"I have had a lot of time to think about all this Doctor, and besides this is a *short* story."

"Indeed."

"Fine with me Doc, I'm sick of this world to be honest, and would be happy to leave, my parents will probably be delighted to get rid of me."

"Well there is another thing that we are hypothesizing about Frond."

"Yeah, wot?"

"Well, it is our understanding that each Dimension, however different, must have the same amount of mass in it as you cannot destroy mass, and all these dimensions whether there is just one or two or many, would have all started from the same Big Bang, so… if we send you to another dimension then we think that it will be a swap. We will get the Frond back from that dimension and you go to the dimension you were supposed to be born into."

"Blimey Mum and Dad will be pleased, but how did this happen Doc?"

"Well, we reckon there is about a 1 and ten billion chance of being born in the wrong dimension, a flux of some kind as you were conceived or a rip in the space time continuum, but you were just unlucky enough for it to be you. So are you happy to do this dimension jump?"

"Whatever."

"Excellent! Sign here," producing clipboard, "here, and... Here!" Splendid, well would you like to speak to anyone, or perhaps write a letter, as we are pretty sure that once you go you won't be coming back, especially as the place you are going to will be the *right* place for you and you won't even *want* to come back!" Smiling with ambitious delight.

"Well, I wouldn't mind speaking to my mum and dad, but that is about it really. I don't have any, er, friends."

"Sure Frond, I'll get them on the phone, we have already been in contact with them, and they know about the basic dimension swap and they are all for it!"

"Oh, well at least I won't be missed." Sighed the lonely girl.

A few moments later Frond found herself in the Black Doctors office on the phone to her dad.

"...so, dad this is it I suppose, I think I'm kinda sorry to go, thanks for all the good stuff we did, but there wasn't a great deal, so I'm not worried I am going to miss anything, and I hope the real me you get will make you and mum happy."

"Thanks for bring so understanding Frond," Said Derek, "You have to understand that your mother and I do love you, but well, we feel that you're the cuckoo in our nest, the Doctor tells us that you're not even our real daughter cause your DNA doesn't match, Oh! Speaking of match, what's the score love? What? Hang on? Listen Frond, I've got to go, the match has started. Good luck in the next dimension, bye." Frond sighed as her dad lost interest in the last conversation he would ever have with his only 'daughter'.

"Hello Frond," began Frond's mum. "Listen, I just want to say that sometimes I do feel for you not fitting in, but now we know it wasn't our fault, I am glad that you are going away. Oh! I mean going to a better place. You see? It's for your own good! You will be happy there, and we will be happier without you."

"I do understand mum."

"Good girl, well good luck, good bye."

"Goodbye mum." Frond put the receiver down and felt a cold wet slug crawl into her empty stomach.

As much as she knew she didn't fit in, there was a certain amount of comfort to be derived from familiar surroundings and tradition, and now she realised that her familiar surroundings of a mum and dad didn't give two hoots about her, and she guessed that her room had already been cleaned out.

She felt sad. It wasn't going to be like going on holiday she thought, because she wouldn't come back and she didn't need a suitcase.

Frond finished writing her little note, which thanked her mum and dad for feeding her and thanked Mr. Erik for listening to her, then she turned out the light and went to sleep.

Tomorrow was going to be a big day.

Chapter 7

Late Breakfast.

Tomorrow was a Wednesday, and traditionally for Frond, Wednesdays had been marginally more acceptable than other school days as she started school with double art, which meant she could kinda-sorta sit by herself and draw and draw.

She thought now that perhaps because she was in the wrong dimension, that that was why her drawings always turned out to be so unlike what she had planned to draw in the first place. But then it occurred to her that she might actually just be crap at art.

The Black Doctor had told Frond that to avoid confusion she should just refer to this Dimension as dimension 'A', just because this was the dimension where she started off, and that predictably, she should refer to the destination dimension as dimension 'B' so that everyone could keep track of who was talking about what dimension.

And more importantly, pointed out the Doctor, so that no one sent anyone to the wrong, ha, ha, Dimension. Because we wouldn't want that now would we?

Frond wandered down from the breakfast room still munching on a soggy triangle of eggy toast. She left little splatters of yellow yolk on the spotless white corridor floor.

The yellow splodges reminded her of dogs wee-ing in the snow, which made her laugh and generally cheered her up a bit.

Then she thought about leaving dimension 'A' and she got all worried again.

When Frond arrived back at her room, the Black Doctor and two nurses were waiting for her. Frond put the eggy toast face down on the bed, just because she could, and knew she didn't have to clear it up.

One for the revolution, she thought.

"Hello," said Frond, "come to send me off eh?" She smiled.

"Frond," said the Doctor, "Try to think of it as us sending you home after a long time away. Anyway, yes it is time, you need to get ready."

One of the nurses handed Frond a white paper surgical gown and a pair of similar material'd slippers.

Frond dressed into them behind the curtain and met the Doctor and Nurses outside her room a moment later.

"I'm ready," she said, annoyed with herself for feeling nervous.

The four of them walked along the corridor back over Frond's eggy drips and eventually turned through another door and along corridors that Frond had yet to travel along before.

After several more doors and a lift and a heavy blast door guarded by two uniformed guards that Frond noticed had guns on their belts, they arrived at a large red double doors.

"Here we are!" said the Doctor and pressing his palm against a metal box on the wall the two doors swished open.

Chapter 8

The flatlines flatlined flatly.

Frond gasped.

The room beyond the doors was enormous.

The biggest room Frond had ever been in was probably the sports hall at school or on a trip to the British Museum, but this was huge! It was the size of a master villains hideout, complete with men in white lab coats with clipboards, with men in military uniforms standing behind glass walls.

In the middle of this Olympic sized room, stood a huge machine.

What a machine! H. G. Wells would have cried to see such a thing and Jules Verne would have fainted. Dr. Frankenstein would have said that there was too much lightning all coming out the top and Steven Spielberg would have been upset that he hadn't already put it in to one of his films.

"Wow!" said Frond, as she turned her head this way and that to take in the vastness and complexity of the Dimension Jumper.

"Blimey and "Crumbs" she suggested. "Fuck me!" She finally offered.

"Frond!" Scolded one of the Nurses.

"Well, I'm sorry, but I mean, well, fuck me!" Apologized Frond.

The Nurse gave her a stern look but said no more, her part in the story having come to an end.

The Black Doctor took Frond by the hand and led her to a strange capsule made of blue plastic glass. Inside was a large amount of viscous foam.

You need to sit in this Frond, and the foam will fill the gaps until you are completely held in place. It won't hurt and you will breathe through this little face mask.

"OK," said Frond, her adrenalin beginning to kick in and her excitement also making an appearance.

Frond climbed up the metal stair and stepped into the blue pod. It made a 'squit' sound which made Frond and a few of the less cultured staff members laugh. Frond made it make another 'squit' sound just for further effect, then she sat down which made a huge fart sound, which had everyone, including the four star General from NASA titter like a child.

"Now put this on," Said the Doctor, offering Frond the face mask.

"Do I get any last words?" Asked Frond?

"Oh, If you would like to. *Now* is the time."

"I just want to say, that I am not afraid to be sent off to this dimension. I think I am glad to leave this place that has been so unkind to me…"

"Actually Frond, we are a bit pressed for time, there's someone from the government here, and well, you know schedules, Tut!" The Black Doctor pressed firmly down on Frond's shoulders pushing her into her blue pod, creating a sound that put a tear in the four star General's eye.

"If home is where you are happy, then I want to go home!" Shouted Frond, as the pod was sealed and the final few buttons were pressed.

The steel stairs were withdrawn and the blue pod rose to its point of optimum dimension jumping. Frond could hardly be seen at all amidst the vast array of lights, scaffolding, machines, thingies and whatnots.

The Doctor and the Nurse who was still in the story, (not the other Nurse, who had already left), hurried off behind a plasteel screen and looked at dials and other complicated machines.

There was a moment of silence and then a low whining sound of machinery coming up to speed then a louder popping sound and eventually a huge ripping sound as the very fabric of the space time continuum was ripped apart, then the sound of a very sticky drain being emptied followed by a camel with really bad diarrhea, then a flash of Saint Elmo's fire that would have made Dr. Frankenstein if he was still around after inspecting the dimension jumper, give a standing ovation, then a 'pop' and all was still.

The Doctor looked at the Nurse and the General looked at his staff. The man from the government looked at the General, who then looked at the Doctor. The nurse looked at the Doctor, who looked at his machine. The man from the government came over and looked at the machine, as did the General. The Machine didn't look at anyone.

"She's gone." Said the Doctor looking at the machine with Frond's name stenciled on the top. It had all sorts of medical pulse monitoring equipment things on it and all of them were reading zero.

The flatlines flatlined flatly.

Chapter 9

Dimension Gate.

"Lower the pod!" Commanded the General.

Amid much creaking and whining the pod was detached and lowered to where only moments before, Frond, had bravely tried to say a few last words.

As the pod was lowered it became apparent that is was not empty. Movement could be seen within, but not clearly, due to the blueness of the glass.

The blue pod was placed in its restraining holder and gradually the hatch opened. A slosh of fluidy fluid flooded out as the Black Doctor approached.

Flopping out of the blue pod came a mewling many tentacled slipping, sliding, suckered vision of damnation. It slid onto the gantry causing the staff to gasp as one, and take a step back.

The thing that replaced Frond looked like a starfish that had been through a paper shredder, it raised a tentacle and screeched a high noted screech that tore into the very soul of everyone who could hear. It was a screech of pain and sadness and of despair.

BLAM! BLAM! And BLAM! BLAM! Again. The four star General dispatched the thing in the only way his tiny mind could muster.

"I told you, you were messing with things you shouldn't mess with," said the General. "You'll get no more funding from the US".

The Doctor, barely able to hold back his tears approached the creature.

The Nurse stood over the expired thing. A white coat wearing scientist, holding his clip board limply by his side, joined them.

"Where, where, what happened to the little girl?" he stuttered out to the Nurse.

"I think we sent her to dimension 'c'," was all she could muster.

"It's worse than that." Spoke the Doctor. Taking a pen from his top pocket he prodded the inert thing and showed his pen top to the nurse.

"What is it Doctor? Pus?"

"No, sister, I think it's eggy toast."

The End

THE BETA CREWS

Introduction:

I wrote this whilst waiting for a train at Paddington station with an incredible hang over - (me not the train) and it all came out in one go, which was a bit like my guts.

You can tell I wrote it a while ago, as it's called 'The Beta Crews' and now it should probably be called 'The HD crews' or 'The 4K Crews', but I kinda' like the sound of 'The Beta Crews'…

I often find it very helpful to write a short film - or even one of my features into a basic story first, dialogue can be distracting, and a false indication of how long your movie is. I realize everyone writes differently, but this way works for me, so I write the story first and generally add the dialogue later, sometimes after work-shopping (I hate that word unless it is used in the context of light engineering, but workshop none the less) it with actors.

I absolutely love this story, but haven't made it into a movie or full short story, and doubt I will.

THE BETA CREWS

In a bleak interview room, on a chair, sits a nervous man.

He fidgets and blinks around. He has an ugly bruise on his forehead and matted blood on his temple and in his hair.

In the corner of the room stands an armed guard.

The man explains that they really should let him go so that he can go and sort out the problem.

A distinguished gentleman from some government Ministry comes to see him, and asks him to tell his story.

Well, says the man and he goes on to explain that it all started when he was sitting in Paddington station nursing a particularly nasty hangover, whilst waiting for a train, and he saw one of those beta crew TV camera units, you know two men and a big shoulder camera, a Sony 900, he says, and he thought , what on Earth are they filming? So he gets up and asks them, and they just stare at him, and walk off.

He thought nothing of it , and as the train is arriving he gets on and goes home.

The next day he sees another crew filming some buildings, and wonders what it is that they are filming, As he walks through London, he sees more and more crews, all two men, one with a camera and one with a clipboard.

So he goes to ask one of them, what is it exactly that they are filming, and they just stare at him as if he is mad, and then they walk off.

At this point the man really begins to wonder, none of the crews seem to have BBC or ITV written on them so he can't phone anyone, his wife thinks he is mad, as he is becoming a bit obsessed about the whole thing.

One day he sees a crew filming the building in which he is working, and he rushes out to find out why. He goes up to them and demands to know why they are filming his building. They just stare at him, then they walk off, Now the man is annoyed and he runs off after them, they get into a car and drive off.

This time he has them - as he notes down the registration plate.

He manages to find out which company the car belongs to and on his lunch hour he sets off to the building, which turns out to be a very non-descript Big office building with no sign outside.

He goes into the reception and asks to see someone about the filming.

He gets a blank stare. The filming he says again, and explains his case. The receptionist asks him to wait.

After a while a tall man came out to talk. He sat down and asked the man all sorts of questions about which particular crews he was talking about and where he had seen them filming.

This is a bit odd thought the man, as he just really wanted the name of the programme. The tall man finally asks the man for his address and said he will send him a copy of the film when it is finished. The man asks what the film is called, and all the man says that they haven't got a definite name for it yet but will keep him informed and thanks for his interest.

The man goes home and notices several beta crews on the way home, and once again they don't seem to be actually filming anything in particular, just buildings and towers and statues. Odd he thinks very odd.

When he arrives home he finds that his house has been broken into and his wife has been really rather badly beaten.

He rushes her to hospital, where he watches her disappear through the bleak surgery doors.

As he waits to hear what has happened to his wife he looks out of the window and sees that there is a beta crew filming the front of the church across the street.

Inside the man, he feels a rage begin to build, but he is on the whole a calm man, so he goes over to the lift and travels down to the ground floor where he walks out to the Beta crew, and just as he gets to them he rushes forward and lays into them, he grabs the beta cam from off the shoulder of the camera man, and smashes it on the floor, with the broken camera he assaults the reporter, whilst kicking the downed cameraman, All rather nasty really.

As is expected the man is detained by the Hospital security, He explains that it was the beta crew, or at least one of them who had beaten up his wife.

The doctor shakes his head sadly and tells the man that his wife has slipped away, and that he is very sorry.

The doctor also goes on to say that the Beta Crew the man assaulted have disappeared without lodging any charges or calling the police so he is free to go.

The man goes home, and finds a message on his answer phone that he is no longer required at his job. And that his p45 is in the post.

He looks out of his window and sees the very same car that he once wrote the number plate down from, pull up outside the front of his house and two men get out. They are not carrying a Beta Cam, and are of a far more aggressive stance than the usual boys.

Our man slips quietly out of the back door and runs off down the street.

He wanders around for a while, trying to think what to do. Eventually he arrives at his friends house who lets him in and says that he can stay.

In the middle of the night the man awakes with intent. He creeps out of his friend's house pausing only to take, a black jacket, a beach towel and a large kitchen knife.

The man travels across town to the building where he met the tall man. It is very late and the building is completely dark, there does not appear to be any security.

With the aid of his towel, the man, jumps and climes over some nasty pointed railings and jumps down onto a basement window. He quietly breaks this and enters the building. He finds himself in some sort of boiler room, and quickly makes his way up through the building to the ground floor and then to the first floor. He forgot to bring a torch which makes things difficult. To make himself less jumpy he takes the knife out of his belt and continues his search. He peers into several rooms but can find nothing except office rooms and editing suites.

He turns a corner and finds a security door with an electronic lock. He is slightly beyond caring now and simply sticks his knife into the lock and after a moments electrical fizzing the door catch is released he enters.

The room contains many TV screens and a central circular table of a highly sophisticated nature. The man looks around in the hope of finding something interesting and sees a file left on a desk, he opens and his breath escapes. He sits down heavily.

Inside the file are the plans of a huge population-moving space craft with huge agricultural pods and domiciles. It appears to be a colony ship from earth to a distant star.

He reads further and discovers that the Beta Crews are filming all the buildings so that all the information can be entered into a central computer and an entire three dimensional holographic of the city can be reproduced so that the colonist will feel at home, and won't be so prone to flipping out and going space ape bonkers.

The man also notices that they are only filming all the nice attractive and aesthetically pleasing buildings and not all the ugly council towers...

Blimey thinks the man. But why do these colonists want to do everything so secretly? What is it that they are hiding from the public?

The man, looks through further files and his eye is caught by the blinking cursor of a computer screen, the computer is still on. He creeps over and moves the mouse, the screen flickers into life, and he looks at the files.

Once he has fiddled around for a moment or two he manages to call up an equation and a graph that seems to indicate that a pollution/greenhouse catastrophe of some complicated nature is imminent. Hence the evacuation of the planet for all the 'A' people.

The man is somewhat stunned at this realization, and as he ponders this, a torch light illuminates his face and several armed guards rush in. In his panic he foolishly uses his kitchen knife. and receives a rifle butt in the face.

The man wakes and finds himself sitting in a chair in an interview room.

He explains that they really should let him go so that he can go and sort out the problem.

The End.

VERY SHORT STORIES

As you probably know 2014 is the centenary of the beginning of WW1.

I'm not sure we should be celebrating it, but we should certainly be remembering it.

This is my little story about WW1, in the form of one letter from a soldier at the front back to his parents back home in England.

3rd of June 1916
Somewhere in France.

Dear Dad,

Yesterday we lost 2nd signals, and my regiment took a pounding. I don't know if you remember Will, who used to work in the orchard at the end of the brook? But he was with them when a squadron of Fokker's descended.

He was a nice bloke and I shall miss him. But I've seen so many nice blokes go already that sometimes, sometimes when I check to see who is still here and whom we have...lost, after an assault, sometimes I feel that I no longer see…people, I see only blood and guts wrapped in soft skin. And sooner or later that skin is burst or scorched or torn and the blood and guts flow...

It's funny really, when the Jasta squadron came out of the sun, I couldn't take my eyes off them, they were so colourful and moved so gracefully, I couldn't really believe that they were instruments of death.

A gun is an ugly thing, a grenade: a ball of grey steel, but a tri-plane? Is it not a thing of beauty? It's just a giant dragonfly. Maybe that's why pilots call their 'crates' she. Like a woman, it can be beautiful, but has the power to cause you great pain, even take the life out of you.

When I last saw you, that day at the pub on the green, I was so excited to get out of the village and head off into the great wide world, but almost a year later, what have I seen in this great wide world of ours?

I've seen the inside of a ship for months at a time, I've seen my best friends green with sea sickness and I have seen them blue with cold and red with blood. Sometimes their own blood. Sometimes the bloody of our enemy and sometimes even my blood.

My blood. That's what I want to talk to you about Dad. My blood.

I'm sorry I haven't written, but you won't believe me when I tell you how hard it is to get paper, a pen or a space that I can write in that isn't stinking, soaking or swamp. It's been so cold lately, that I feel if I exposed my fingers to hold a pen and write, it might be the last thing I do. Several of the lads have lost a finger to frost bite, but as long as it isn't a trigger finger, no one seems to mind.

I think when me and the lads left to fight for 'King and Country', I think we all thought that we'd be back in a few weeks or months and it will have all been a jolly good bash up. But I think now, that if any of us had had any idea what it was going to be like, we would have all gone and hid like Jones' son did. How we laughed at him then and how I wish I had the courage to say 'no' like he did, now.

Most importantly, Dad, I thought I was going to be back within nine months.

At night, I can hear them: the Krauts, just yards from were we rot. They sing and laugh, just like us. But when I see one I have to shoot him. It is my duty to try to kill him in whatever way I can. Once they threw over a tin of salt beef. It was the best dinner we had had for days, until our company sergeant found us and made us throw it back. Bloody stupid.

I keep thinking about Mum's roast beef. What I'd do to even smell that is unimaginable. Do you remember the farewell dinner Mum cooked for? Do you remember Jenny the little redheaded girl I introduced to you? The Daughter of Mr. and Mrs. Thompson? She had a blue dress on and green eyes?

Well, I wonder if you have seen her since that evening. Because you might have noticed a change.

We haven't had any change here for a month. Except for a constant change of faces, as new faces arrive and old faces get blown off or decay into the mud. I try not to make friends, as it is easier to grieve for someone you didn't really know or like, than for a friend. If I grieved every time someone close to me had died, I would be a shell.

I saw a snail the other day. A tiny speck of life in this desolate, dead, dead place. I couldn't help but smile. I almost climbed out of my foxhole to look more closely at it, and as I watched entranced by its slow moving almost timeless existence, a bird swooped down out of the sky and plucked it from the branch it was crawling along.

Its beak scooping out the snail's flesh and discarding its shell like an unwanted soul.

There are a lot of unwanted souls discarded around here. But there is one soul I do want. And this is where you come in Dad.

I really thought I'd be back in time to tell you and Mum in due time, but I don't think that's going to happen. You see, me and Jenny have been courting for a while, and just before I went she told me she was pregnant. I knew you and Mum would be disappointed, what with us not being married and all. But I love Jenny, and just a few days ago, I got a letter from her to say, that I'm now you Dad: I'm a Dad.

We are going to call him Thomas and I want him to have your name for his middle name. I want you to love him and treat him like your real grandson, and I know that when you see him you will love him, even if you don't approve of how he was bought into the world.

If I was there I'd marry Jenny and all would be well. But I'm not there Dad, and there's no one else to ask to look after my little Jenny and my little Thomas. And I'm not going to be there Dad. Not ever. I'm not even where you think I am.

There was some heavy shelling three days ago, and a gas attack. The jawbone of my corporal shattered the cylinder on my gas mask, after he took a piece of shrapnel in the face.

I tried to grab his gasmask, but got several lung-full's of chlorine gas before I could get it off him and onto me.

The stretcher-bearers got me back to the infirmary, but the doctor gave me one of those looks that I have seen doctors give to people before. Dead people.

He told me that I needed to 'finish anything that wasn't finished'. I didn't know what he meant until he gave me some paper and this here pen.

So I'm in the infirmary. I can feel the fluid filling up my lungs, I've lost count of the amount of times I've had to stop writing this letter because I've been coughing too much, or I dropped the pen.

The nurse says that the chlorine has got into my lungs and that it irritates the lungs inner lining, so that they can't take in any oxygen and kills off all the cells. I watched a man in the next bunk drown earlier today. Like a fish on the shore. His eyes looking up to see what? A God? If there is a God then he isn't here.

To say 'in God we trust'. Well aren't we praying to the same God as the Krauts?

In Dulce Decorum Est, they said. Well there is nothing fitting and proper about living and dying like this, but at least in some small way, I have bought life into this world as well as death.

Dad, please promise me that will look after Jenny and little Thomas, I've never really asked for anything and I'm sorry if you feel I let you down. I love you and I love Mum, I hope my son, your grandson, might fill the gap I leave.

Love

Your son

Martin. x

VERY SHORT STORIES 2

In contrast to the story above I thought I'd write a story from the father to the son (rather than the other way round). Same date – but 90 years later in a very different world, a different time, and quite a different matter…

3rd of June 2006
Death Row.

Dear Michael,

Your mother and I felt that we had a few things that we wanted you to know that we had just not been able to tell you during the last few months.

It's been very difficult to get to talk to you, and every time we have been able to speak with you face to face their has always been some uniformed guards confusing us and stopping us from saying what it is we really wanted to say.

You know your mother had a problem communicating with Mr. Stephens, your lawyer, but then I suppose it is only natural that a man like him would be such a nasty piece of work when he spends his whole life defending the very scum of the world, that decent people like your mother and I want to be protected from. And indeed pay our taxes, that we have earned with the sweat of our brow and the bend of our spines to defend. What a twisted world we live in.

Mr. Stephens informed us the other day that your final appeal has been turned down, he was quite carefree in the way he told us that there was absolutely no further avenue to pursue. They are going to put you, our son, to death for the crimes you have committed. I felt like he was telling me my library book was overdue, not informing me of the imminent death of our only child.

But then. On the way out of the courtroom last month we were ushered into a police van, to avoid the press. Your mother was in tears and by the time I had finished comforting her and wiping away her tears, realised that we were sitting opposite Mr. and Mrs. Beck.

You remember them? Maybe not. Let me refresh your memory. They are the parents, or in fact *were* the parents of the girl you raped and killed.

They just stared at us the Becks. I didn't know what to say, what could I say? The police officers on each side of us, could see that they had maybe made a slight faux pas, putting us both in the same van, but then it was a spur of the moment thing, as the press of journos had got so great they had to get us out somehow.

Your Mother went and sat next to Mrs. Beck, hugged her and they just cried. They cried and cried.

I have never felt so useless in my life. You made me feel like that.

You.

My son.

The child I have suffered for. I have slaved for. The child who I have fed and clothed. Looked after when sick. The child of whom I have never asked anything.

And how have you re-paid us?

The house has been sold now and we will be moving the day after your… well the day after you go.

We've lived in that house for 27 years, but your mother felt that you had tainted the house and she felt she couldn't live with the looks from the neighbours.

She's right. I've seen it. I've walked into the paper shop and heard the voices hush, and caught the fragmented sentence. "…He's the father of…", "the boy who raped that girl,". I don't think for a moment you have considered how far reaching your evil acts were. You have polluted not only your own life but also the life of your poor victim, her family and friends, her school colleagues. And our family, your own flesh and blood.

YOUR OWN FLESH AND BLOOD.

How can our lives ever be the same again?

The police showed us the photos. We saw what you did. In fact half the country saw what you did as it was in all the newspapers and there was even a special report on Newsnight. I always felt that one day you would be a household name but I could never have dreamed in my darkest, sickest nightmare that it would be for this.

Where did we go wrong? What did we fail to do that made you turn into a monster capable of … well I don't think I need to write again what it was that has damned your soul for eternity.

We are moving to a little village to the west of Glastonbury. I don't feel the need to tell you the name of the village because you won't ever be coming to visit and I don't want anyone who may find this letter to have an indication. We have been hounded enough. Night after night of having the press outside our front door.

What did they think they were going to see? It's not as if we have another child who can 'perform' for them.

That photograph of you smiling on the courtroom steps as you were led in on the first day of the trail, has become somewhat iconic you'll probably be interested to know. The Guardian ran it with the line "Stare into the face of Death", and the Sun said "Smile Please." What upset you mother the most is that it took so long for you to be caught and that the police only ever managed to track you down because of the photographs you took.

To imagine that we had dinner with you and watched TV with you, talked to you, washed your clothes, lent you the car, and all the while you had this dark shadow spreading from you like an oil slick in pure water and all the while that beautiful girl was slowly rotting into the bottom of the lake.

How you could ever smile and how you could live is an anathema to us all.

I want you to know that we are not worried about losing our son as we don't and never have had a son.

We hope you burn in hell.

We despise you.

Goodbye.

Mum and Dad.

GRAPHIC NOVELS & COMICS

I read a lot of graphic novels and comics, and would love to write them, but the way in is even smaller than the way into movies!

Only one UK comic – 2000AD!

So I wrote a couple of short scripts for Tharg the alien editor of 2000AD (and the Megazine).

But he never got back to me – one day I will get a full length comic published!

Here are a couple of ideas for short graphic novels, Sounds Sinister written as a synopsis, and Underground Workers as a fully realized comic strip and with all the words written in comic script format!

SOUNDS SINISTER

Whilst at work one day a Radio DJ finds an alien tape…

Synopsis:

Picture of Sound technician in Sound studio. Piles of tapes, CD's, reels etc.

A technician sorting through a pile of pop records and tapes in preparation for a radio show finds an un-labelled spool, annoyed at this lack of professionalism thinks that he'd better check it, and pops it in the slot, bungs on some headphones and flicks the switch.

He is immediately thrown into a trance like state, almost a coma. Until with a sudden click the tape ends, and he wakes up, he shakes his head in disbelief, he feels wonderful.

He checks the file but just cannot find out whose tape this is. He asks a colleague who is equally mystified, and after some serious searching, they reason that as it isn't labeled, they should use it anyway, perhaps who ever owns it will recognize it when they hear it?

There is a bit of a disagreement between those who see danger in its use and those who see its money potential, the latter of course win.

The music is subsequently played on the radio, with an appeal for the composer to come forward.

The country is thrown into chaos as 1000's of people fall in to trance like states, whilst driving, climbing ladders, performing operations. Disaster!

The station is flooded with requests for more plays and addresses of retailers, also death threats from angry relatives of those killed during the transmission.

The Government bans the playing of it, and the police seize the tape.

But inevitably through home taping, tapes appear on the black market, and are sold at incredibly high prices, the trance like state is highly sought after.

Meanwhile in a top secret Government research lab, the boffins analyze the tape and find that it has sound forms and waves of an Un-earthly origin.

The fuss gradually dies down, but the tapes are still out there, and who knows what pro-longed exposure to them may develop.

A sample tape is delivered to the military for investigation as a weapon.

Meanwhile the original Technician who was sacked from the radio station, is now working at a TV company, thinking, thank god that is all over.

He is sorting through a pile of video cassette and tapes in preparation for a TV show, and finds an unlabelled video, annoyed at this lack of professionalism he thinks that he better check it, and pops it in the slot, bungs on some headphones and flicks the switch...

The End

Underground Workers

This was written as I was sitting on the tube waiting for it to move – and over the tannoy the mechanical voice said the delay was due to underground workers.

It didn't say what they had or hadn't done, just that it was their fault!

As you can see the final illustrated comic is only 3 pages long, and the script was five, so a bit of editing did occur, but all the better for it!

I had hoped that Tharg would have been interested, he wasn't so I found a wonderful artist, Vicky Stonebridge, who was interested in illustrating it – and it was published in Future Quake magazine, but sadly Tharg still wasn't interested.

Damn his green Betelgeuseian hide.

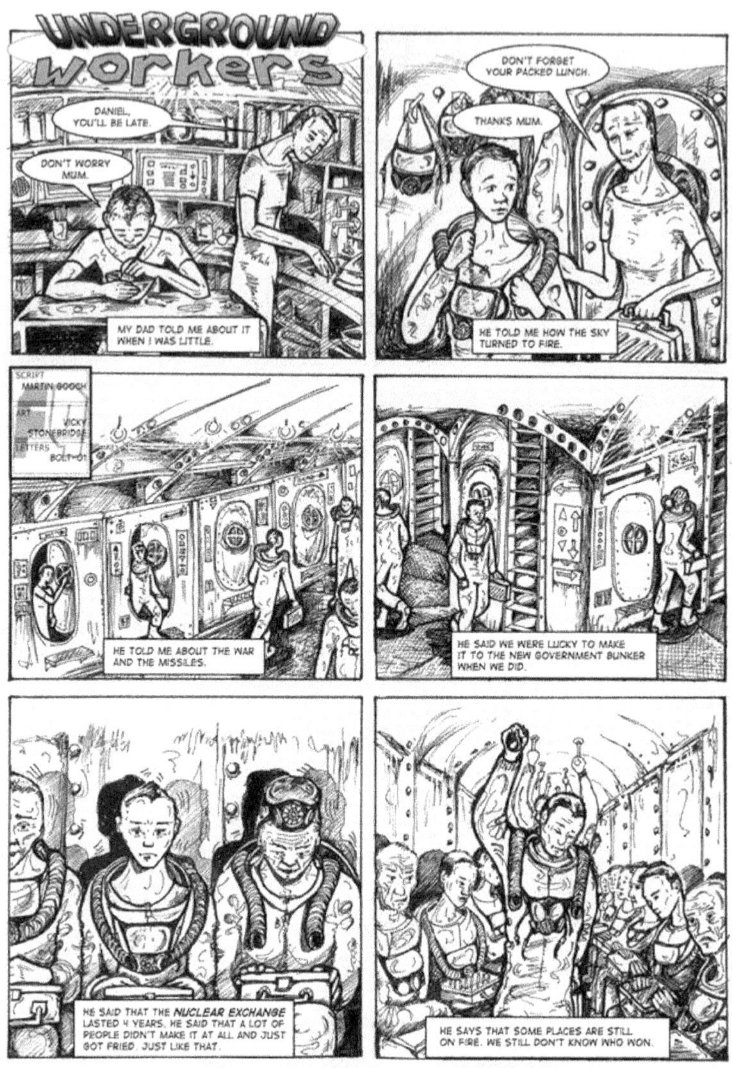
UNDERGROUND workers
DANIEL, YOU'LL BE LATE.
DON'T WORRY MUM.
MY DAD TOLD ME ABOUT IT WHEN I WAS LITTLE.
DON'T FORGET YOUR PACKED LUNCH.
THANKS MUM.
HE TOLD ME HOW THE SKY TURNED TO FIRE.
SCRIPT MARTIN GOOCH
ART VICKY STONEBRIDGE
LETTERS BOLT-01
HE TOLD ME ABOUT THE WAR AND THE MISSILES.
HE SAID WE WERE LUCKY TO MAKE IT TO THE NEW GOVERNMENT BUNKER WHEN WE DID.
HE SAID THAT THE NUCLEAR EXCHANGE LASTED 4 YEARS. HE SAID THAT A LOT OF PEOPLE DIDN'T MAKE IT AT ALL AND JUST GOT FRIED. JUST LIKE THAT.
HE SAYS THAT SOME PLACES ARE STILL ON FIRE. WE STILL DON'T KNOW WHO WON.

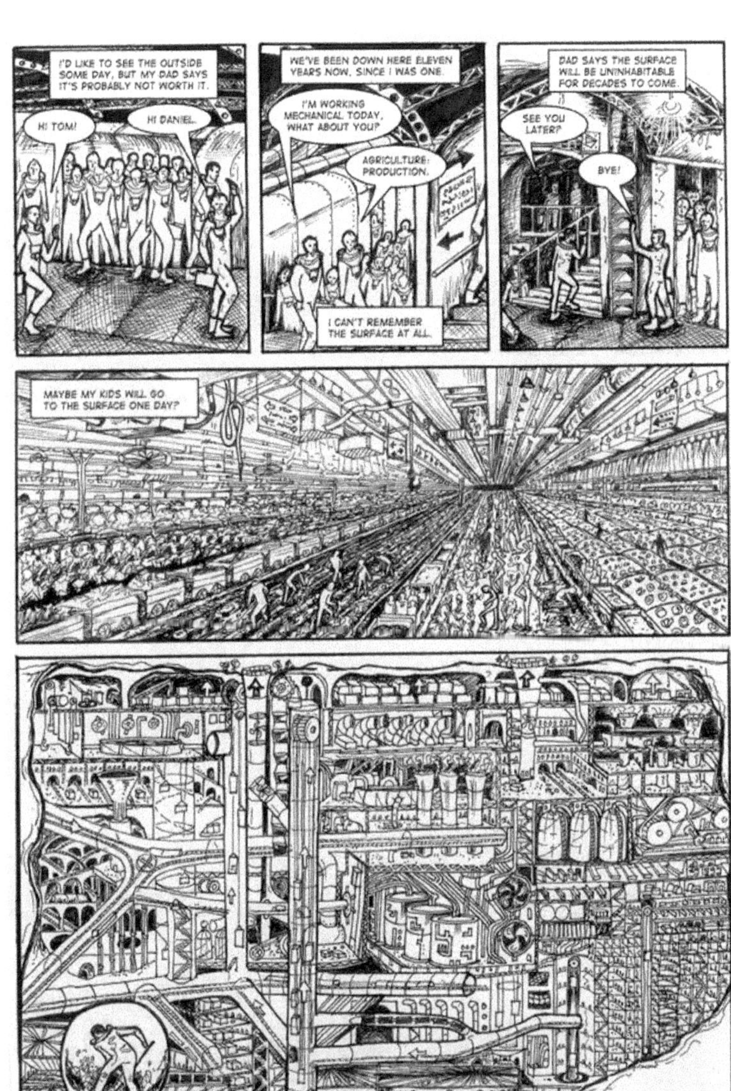
I'D LIKE TO SEE THE OUTSIDE SOME DAY, BUT MY DAD SAYS IT'S PROBABLY NOT WORTH IT.
HI TOM!
HI DANIEL.
WE'VE BEEN DOWN HERE ELEVEN YEARS NOW, SINCE I WAS ONE.
I'M WORKING MECHANICAL TODAY, WHAT ABOUT YOU?
AGRICULTURE: PRODUCTION.
I CAN'T REMEMBER THE SURFACE AT ALL.
DAD SAYS THE SURFACE WILL BE UNINHABITABLE FOR DECADES TO COME.
SEE YOU LATER?
BYE!
MAYBE MY KIDS WILL GO TO THE SURFACE ONE DAY?

DON'T YOU EVER FEEL GUILTY ABOUT SENDING ALL THOSE POOR PEOPLE UNDERGROUND?
GUILT? WE SAVED THE HUMAN RACE DEAR BOY.
THE COUNTRY WAS FILLING UP, CRIME WAS APPALING, DISEASE WAS ON THE RISE.
A FEW SPECIAL EFFECTS AND A FEW WELL-PLACED EXPLOSIONS AND THEY ALL WENT WILLINGLY UNDERGROUND.
BUT WAS THAT FAIR?
WHAT'S FAIR GOT TO DO WITH IT?
I SUPPOSE SO...
THE END

UNDERGROUND WORKERS: THE SCRIPT

Page 1

Page 1 Panel 1

We see a boy (Daniel, about 12 years old) eating his breakfast in a slightly futuristic kitchen, but it is pretty shabby and has NO WINDOWS. The ceiling is low and it isn't very nice. Daniel's mum is washing up. They both have slightly futuristic clothing.

MUM: DANIEL! YOU'LL BE LATE!

DANIEL: DON'T WORRY MUM.

CAPTION: MY DAD TOLD ME ABOUT IT WHEN I WAS LITTLE.

Page 1 Panel 2

We see Daniel putting his coat on by the front door, it is like a radiation suit and has a facemask. His mum stands next to him.

She has his packed lunch box.

MUM: DON'T FORGET YOUR PACKED LUNCH

DANIEL: THANKS MUM.

CAPTION: HE TOLD ME ABOUT HOW THE SKY TURNED TO FIRE.

Page 1 Panel 3

Daniel comes out of his 'house'. He is in a big underground bunker type building, but nasty and shabby. There are other people also around, with similar clothing. It is like some horrid underground ghetto. There is no sky or windows only concrete and metal.

Daniel heads off up the 'street'.

CAPTION: HE TOLD ME ABOUT THE WAR AND THE MISSILES.

Page 1 Panel 4

Daniel walks through the underground complex, past more grubby areas.

Caption: He said we were lucky to make it to the new Government bunker when we did.

Page 2

Page 2 Panel 1

Daniel arrives at a transport system of some sort, maybe like a tube train.

CAPTION: HE SAID A LOT OF PEOPLE DIDN'T MAKE IT AT ALL. AND JUST GOT FRIED. JUST LIKE THAT.

Page 2 Panel 2

Daniel is travelling on the 'tube train'. It is packed with loads of grim faced grubby people. Everyone looks sad.

CAPTION: HE SAID THE 'NUCLEAR EXCHANGE' LASTED 4 YEARS.

Page 2 Panel 3

We have a close up of Daniel's face.

CAPTION: HE SAYS THAT SOME PLACES ARE STILL ON FIRE.

Page 2 Panel 4

Daniel is still on the tube. We see some of the other faces on the tube, all miserable and sickly.

CAPTION: WE STILL DON'T KNOW WHO WON.

Page 3

Page 3 Panel 1

The tube train arrives at its stop and they all troop off.

Daniel sees another boy in the crowd waving at him.

BOY: HI TOM!

BOY 2: HI DANIEL.

CAPTION: I'D LIKE TO SEE THE OUTSIDE SOME DAY, BUT MY DAD SAYS IT'S PROBABLY NOT WORTH IT.

Page 3 Panel 2

The two boys walk along another nasty looking tunnel.

DANIEL: WHERE YOU WORKING TODAY?

TOM: IN MECHANICAL. WORKING ON MOTORS.

CAPTION: WE'VE BEEN DOWN HERE ELEVEN YEARS NOW, SINCE I WAS ONE.

Page 3 Panel 3

Daniel arrives at a junction.

TOM: WHAT ABOUT YOU?

DANIEL: AGRICULTURE: PRODUCTION.

CAPTION: I CAN'T REMEMBER THE SURFACE AT ALL.

Page 3 Panel 4

The two boys head different ways.

TOM: SEE YOU LATER?

DANIEL: BYE!

CAPTION: DAD SAYS THE SURFACE WILL BE UNINHABITABLE FOR DECADES TO COME.

Page 4

Page 4 Panel 1

This is a much wider picture of Daniel working in the 'field'. We see it is really huge and there are loads of people working it.

CAPTION: MAYBE MY KIDS WILL BE ABLE TO GO UP TO THE SURFACE ONE DAY?

Page 4 Panel 2

This is like an architects cross section of a building. We see that Daniel is in an underground complex. We see all the different levels. There is a scale showing the size of the complex and we see that Daniel is right at the bottom of level 20, miles below the surface of the planet.

The arrows also show how food production, clothing and mechanical stuff are made in the complex but transported to the surface.

An arrow points us up towards the surface. We follow.

Page 5

Page 5 Panel 1

On the surface of the planet, we are on a nice golf course.

Two very rich looking men are playing golf under a beautiful sky.

GOLFER 1: DON'T YOU EVER FEEL GUILTY ABOUT SENDING ALL THOSE WORKERS UNDERGROUND?

GOLFER 2: GUILT? WE SAVED THE HUMAN RACE DEAR BOY.

Page 5 Panel 2

Golfer 1 hits a great shot, they both squint to see where it went in the beautiful countryside.

GOLFER 2: THE COUNTRY WAS FILLING UP, CRIME WAS APPALLING, DISEASE WAS ON THE RISE. A FEW SPECIAL EFFECTS AND A FEW WELL-PLACED EXPLOSIONS AND THEY ALL WENT WILLINGLY UNDERGROUND.

GOLFER 1: BUT WAS THAT FAIR?

Page 5 Panel 3

The two golfers are walking away from us under a beautiful sky, with birds flying around, nice trees and a church spire in the distance. This is a new Eden!

GOLFER 2: WHAT'S FAIR GOT TO DO WITH IT?

GOLFER 1: I SUPPOSE SO…

The End.

POEMS

POEM 1

Here are my poems,
Some are silly, some are not,
The really good ones,
I forgot.

PEANUT BUTTER

I like peanut butter,
I love it on toast,
I love peanut butter
I love it the most.

DEAD RAT

Dead Rat,

Walking home one day I found a dead rat in the road.

It was stinky and squashed as flat as a wet sock.

Thinking about it - It could've been a toad.

It just lay there in the shadow of a rock.

I wonder if Transport For London will use this in their poems on the tube campaign?

It's not very good, doesn't follow any poetic conventions and doesn't even have that proper rhyming scheme thing.

I'll submit it tomorrow.

The End

www.ingramcontent.com/pod-product-compliance
Ingram Content Group UK Ltd.
Pitfield, Milton Keynes, MK11 3LW, UK
UKHW021051270726
13967UKWH00012B/523